SWORDS
BOOK THREE O

Robert Ryan

Copyright © 2022 Robert J. Ryan
All Rights Reserved. The right of Robert J. Ryan to be identified as the author of this work has been asserted. All of the characters in this book are fictitious and any resemblance to actual persons, living or dead, is coincidental.

Cover design by www.damonza.com

ISBN: 9798843186784
(print edition)

Trotting Fox Press

Contents

1. Food is Strength	3
2. They Pay Well	9
3. The Worst News	15
4. Doubt and Delay	21
5. Lord of the Ahat	30
6. Act of War	38
7. You're Dead	51
8. Respect	59
9. The Conclave	63
10. Unrelenting	71
11. Choose Now	76
12. Queen of the Gods	84
13. The Serpents Strike	93
14. The Swift March	99
15. Blood on Her Hands	109
16. To Wait is to Die	116
17. All Rules Can be Broken	123
18. The Legend	128
19. Let's Speak	135
20. A Dark Current	140
21. The Time of Swords	146
22. The Scream of Swords	153
23. Attack!	159
24. Sorcery Unleashed	165
25. Brothers in Arms	176
26. The Seeds of Revenge	186
Appendix: Encyclopedic Glossary	194

1. Food is Strength

Shar wished she were dead.

At the same time a burning rage flowed through her. She would not die until she had vengeance upon her captor. It was an oath she swore to herself, over and again. She found that thinking about it, imagining that vengeance, took her mind off the pain she endured.

Nerchak headed southwest, and he employed great skill. He avoided any area of human habitation with meticulous care. With even greater care he took trouble to hide their trail. There was a glimmer of hope for Shar though, and when her thoughts were not on dark vengeance they were on Asana and Kubodin. The pony her captor rode, and the one she was tied to, left tracks that could not always be concealed on rocky trails or within running water. There was a path, if a scant one, for her friends to follow.

But it might take days for them to discover it, if they ever did at all. Meanwhile, Nerchak had a lead, and he was the sort of man who did not take chances. He pushed ahead as fast as the ponies could trot, and rests were few and far between.

The days passed by in a blur of pain. Ropes bit into her flesh. Hunger gnawed at her stomach, for he rarely risked feeding her lest she try to escape. Although it seemed to her that this was more a streak of cruelty or an attempt to establish his dominance. He could not fear her when she was bound. If he knew her thoughts though, perhaps he would have.

All the while he headed southwest, and it seemed to Shar that there could be only one destination. Three Moon Mountain. It was the home of the shamans. It was their sacred land. It was their fortress, where even the great emperor had left them in peace during the years of his ascendancy and their banishment.

Three Moon Mountain. None went there save for the shamans. Though rumored stories told tales of prisoners taken to it. None ever came back to confirm it. If she ended up in that place, she would not return either. So she *must* escape.

Nerchak had ensured she could not though. Her wrists were bound. He had struck her many times, and that was intended to mentally intimidate her. And, perhaps, he limited her supply of food and water in order to diminish her physical strength as well.

She would wait though. He was vigilant, but at some point he would make a mistake. When the chance of escape came, she would snatch it.

On one point he had relented. Initially, she had been thrown over the saddle of her pony like a sack and tied to it. That was to dehumanize her, but repeatedly undoing those knots and tying them again took him time, and for one reason or another, he stopped doing that and let her ride with just her wrists bound. Whatever his reason was, it was not based on mercy. He had none.

Nor would she, she vowed, when her chance at escape came.

Daylight of the third day of their flight came, for they only traveled at night now, and Nerchak picked a camping spot. He chose a grassy glade in a thick area of timber, and he gathered some dry wood and lit a small campfire. All the while he left her on the pony, though the agony of sitting there nearly brought her to tears. She was not used to riding.

She did not show it though. And when he finally came to her and checked her bonds, which he did frequently, she was compliant and made no complaint. Even so, he suddenly hauled her off the pony and threw her to the ground. Once there, he kicked her.

Shar did not resist. If he thought she was beaten, he might make a mistake in the way he guarded her. If she tried to fight back, it would only teach him to remain on guard.

He left her then, and she crawled close to the fire. He never let her get too close lest she try to burn the rope that bound her.

The fire burned down to embers, and over this he cooked a simple meal. He offered her no food. Nor did he speak to her. So she sat quiet and still, and dreamed of better times.

After a while he came over. He looked at her briefly, checked her bonds, and then place a bowl of leftover food on the ground.

"Eat," he commanded.

It was another of his games. Her hands were tied behind her back, so she had no way of eating except to grovel like an animal. Yet she did not hesitate. Food was strength, and without either she had no hope of escape. It would also help lull him into the idea that the fight had gone out of her.

He laughed, and the sound of it infuriated her, but there was nothing to be done. When she was finished, he poured a little water into the bowl.

"Drink, *princess*."

She drank, and the water seemed cool and sweet to her. It was the first he had given her since the same time yesterday.

"Get up," he ordered.

She did so, and knew what was coming next. He led her to a tree away from the fire, and he bound her to it securely. He would sleep soon, and he would take no chances. Just binding her hands and feet was not enough, for she might manage to break free. But being tied to the tree prevented all movement. It secured her perfectly, though after a few hours of being unable to move pain would set in again.

She vowed to endure. At the same time, the longer this treatment of beatings, hunger and restraint that left her body aching, the less chance she had of somehow overcoming him when her chance came. If she were to escape, she must make the attempt soon.

Nerchak lay down near the fire, sword in hand. It seemed that he went to sleep quickly. That was good. Despite being ready with the sword, he felt secure enough to ignore her. The tactic of submission that she was employing seemed to be lulling him.

She did not sleep though. She was too uncomfortable, and thirst plagued her. He was not giving her enough water. She felt her anger rise again, but let it fade away. It served no purpose now. When the chance came to escape, she would give it free reign. It would help her tortured body respond.

Her mind drifted in a state of half sleep. She wondered how she had come to this point. Had Nerchak given her any signs that she should have seen?

She cast her mind back over their travels. Always he had seemed older than his appearance. That had been an indicator, along with his skill at swordsmanship. Both showed he had received special training, and she should have pressed him to find out what that was. He had not wanted to go to the Wahlum Hills either. Now, she understood why. That took them away from the destination he had in mind. She could not blame herself for not seeing that though.

Above all there was that look on Drasta's face, the Two Ravens' shaman, before Nerchak killed him. It was one of recognition, and Shar had seen it but foolishly dismissed it. All that had happened to her stemmed from her own errors. Next time, she would not be so trusting.

If there were a next time. The army she was building would already have begun to disintegrate. Who followed a leader who could not look after themselves?

She moved a little as she dozed, and the tight rope around her wrists bit into her flesh. At the same time a fly buzzed her face, and she shook her head several times to scare it away. There would be no sleep now. She was wide awake, and her whole body throbbed while her mouth felt dry as dust.

It was no good feeling sorry for herself. A chance of escape would come, and she must keep herself as strong as possible until then. The future was what counted. Reliving the errors of her past would change nothing.

Somehow, she must have slept for she woke to find it was late afternoon, and Nerchak had saddled the ponies again. She saw that the fire had been rekindled, but had started to die down once more. He had no doubt eaten again, but he had not offered her any food. Nor would he, she thought. Still less the water that she needed even more.

By the time the sun was a red ball of fire on the horizon, they rode ahead through the lengthening shadows of dusk. The air was cooling on Shar's face, and she felt better for it, and also to be moving. No doubt that would soon change as the discomfort of riding grew on her again.

Even as the last of the light faded they came to the crest of a ridge and looked outward. The Wahlum Hills were ending, dropping away in treeless slopes to flat lands below.

"Where to now?" she asked, her voice a croak in her dry throat. She did not want to speak to him, and she dreaded the answer, but morbid curiosity had driven her.

He glanced back at her and smiled. "Not where you think. Somewhere even worse."

2. They Pay Well

They moved out of the misty hills under cover of dark, and Shar missed them. Her friends were there. Her army was there. And it was a place of beauty. Where she headed now there were only enemies and death.

It did not take them long to reach the flat lands below the hills. Here and there they saw the distant lights of villages, but Nerchak avoided these carefully. Whether that was good for her or not, Shar could not decide. If they ran into other people she might be freed. At the same time, anyone who attempted to help her would probably die. Few could stand against Nerchak. As much as she now hated him, she did not forget his skill with a sword. She would not want the deaths of innocents on her conscience.

It was possible that anyone they ran into would want to kill her anyway. Many people saw the shamans as the oppressors they were, but there were some, and no small number, who supported their tyrannical ways. Some received benefit from the shamans, such as nazram. Others had been indoctrinated since youth, for the shamans made a special point of controlling how and what the young were taught.

The night wore on, and several times Shar stifled cries of agony as her pony moved over uneven ground and she shifted into a bad position in the saddle.

She rode in a daze, and so she missed until too late that there were suddenly people nearby. She heard them talking quietly, and she saw the light of torches or lanterns emerge from behind a stand of trees and pass onward in the darkness. Nerchak had not missed them though. He had seen them late however, and there was no chance to back away into the night. Instead, he had come up to her and his knife was against her throat.

"Move or make a sound," he whispered, "and you die."

She believed him. She sat there, silent and still. The procession passed ahead of them, maybe fifty feet away, and whoever it was did not see them in the dark. No doubt the light of the torches took away their night vision.

Shar waited in breathless silence. The procession went ahead, and it seemed to her that they were farmers or woodcutters returning to their village from a late day's work. Even if she did not deliberately try to attract their attention, she still might die. If one of the ponies neighed, it would reveal their presence.

The column of lights went ahead however, and soon they wound away into the distance.

"Good, princess." She felt the cold blade of the knife press harder against her skin, and then it was gone.

They continued forward then through the dark, and it was faster going than in the hills. This was a mostly open grassland, and there were few obstacles. It did seem to be well-populated though, and veering away from villages slowed them down.

That thought did bring back to Shar something that Nerchak had said earlier. She had no wish to talk to him, but knowledge was power.

"Please. What did you mean when you said we weren't going where I thought?"

She spoke quietly, being careful to make sure he would not take her words as any sort of challenge to his authority. She would be submissive now in order to surprise him later.

He slowed his pony a little so hers drew closer. The rope that he used to lead it dangled over the ground, and she wondered if she could make use of that somehow in an attempted escape.

"Tell me where you think we're going," he responded, and even in the dark where she could not see his face properly she detected the amusement in his voice.

"Three Moon Mountain," she replied. It surprised her that she said the words so steadily.

He laughed at that. "Fool. You're playing a game and you don't even know the rules. You don't even know all the other *players*."

That surprised her. She did not think he was lying. Had he wanted to apply more mental pressure against her, he would have confirmed they were going to Three Moon Mountain. Anything other than that was a relief. Of sorts.

"Then why don't you tell me? Who are the other players? What am I missing?"

He looked back at her thoughtfully. So she judged by the delay in his answer at any rate.

"You fear the shamans, and well you should. But a curse upon them, and their ways. However, they do pay well. I've been to Three Moon Mountain, and I suspect there's enough gold there to make a mountain all by itself."

That surprised her again. Not that they hoarded gold there. Shulu had told her it was so. The shamans had stripped the lands of wealth for century after century. What surprised her was that he had been to Three Moon Mountain at all. Unless he was lying.

"You didn't answer my question." She knew as soon as she spoke that she had struck the wrong tone. She had not been meek enough, yet still he only laughed.

"Who wants me, if not the shamans?" she asked, deliberately allowing a little desperation to creep into her voice.

"Truly, I could sell you to the highest bidder. My loyalty lies elsewhere though, and there are other powers in the land as old as the shamans, and maybe more powerful for all that they work in the dark."

It was an answer that was no answer. It was all she was going to get though. He kicked his pony ahead, and the rope lead stretched tight again. She still wondered if she could use that somehow, but there might be a better way if the right situation arose.

She turned her mind to his answer. What other powers were there? There were the shamans, the clan chiefs and the nazram. None of those worked in the dark though. Their power was clear and obvious, so he could not mean them.

It made no sense. Shulu had certainly never mentioned any other powers in the land. And she would have known of their existence if such a group existed, no matter how secret. Then again, great as her grandmother's powers were, she was not infallible. It might be that she had missed something.

Shar kept thinking on it, but no answers came to her. If they were out there, she would have to wait. Perhaps she would only discover the truth when Nerchak had reached whatever destination he traveled to. By then, though, it would be too late. She must escape before then, but if she did the mystery he posed would remain unsolved.

Escape. It was a thought that ran constantly across her mind, but she had to ensure she never gave a hint of her intention. He must know that she would try, but the longer she lulled him the greater the chance he would make a mistake anyway. Part of that was not trying anything too early. She could not take a half chance. She must not let desperation force her hand. She would have one opportunity only, and when a good one came she must grasp at it with everything, and risk her life. Death here and now would be infinitely preferable to whatever further captors he intended to hand her over to.

However much she hoped though, he did not seem lulled at all. He looked back often to check her bonds visually, and from time to time he dismounted to check them by hand, tightening them as necessary.

There was another bad sign too. Now that they had left the hills he stopped and rested more frequently. That could only mean one thing. He no longer feared any pursuit. In truth, she had long given up on whatever slim hope there was for that. She knew Asana and Kubodin would not abandon her, but since the beginning of her abduction it was obvious they would not be able to find her trail, or if they did they would be too far behind to effect a rescue.

No matter. The blood of the emperor ran in her veins, and she would find a way to escape by herself.

They plodded on through the night, and as usual the pain in Shar's body grew. Her hands were numb from poor circulation, and the rest of her ached. She could not take much more of this, and she had begun to flinch every time Nerchak approached. He only smiled at that, and it should have made her furious. But her mind was growing as numb as her hands.

At some point she dozed in the saddle and was startled by a punch to her side.

"Get off," Nerchak ordered.

She was not sure what was happening, but she tried to dismount, clumsy as she was with her hands tied behind her back. It was not fast enough for Nerchak and he heaved her off and threw her to the ground, the hilt of one of her swords digging into her body harshly.

A few moments later she realized why. He was swapping mounts with her, and when he had retied the lead rope and they were both mounted again, she knew instantly that her pony, his old one, was going lame.

He might have made the change because she was lighter and less a burden on the pony, but more likely he just wanted the best mount in case he was forced to flee an attack. If so, he was not quite as confident as he appeared.

Her hip ached where the hilt had dug in, and that gave her an idea. Through the pain, her mind fixed on that.

3. The Worst News

Asana woke, and he knew instantly something was wrong.

Light came into his hut through the smoke hole at the peak of the roof. It was dawn, or not long after. He rolled up from the furs that formed his bed on the floor, and his sword was in his hand before he even realized he had grasped it.

There he waited, poised and ready for action, but listening to try to determine what was going on. He could not tell. There was certainly a commotion outside, and yelling. There did not seem to be any attack going on though.

He put down the sword and took the time to put on his boots. When he was done, he reached for the sword again and even as he did a voice called out to him through the hide door that closed off his hut.

"Asana!"

It was Kubodin. Something was very wrong.

Quickly, he pulled open the hide door and walked out into the early morning sun.

Kubodin wasted no time. "Shar's gone."

"Gone where?"

"Taken. Abducted. We don't know where."

Asana felt a deep sense of unease. Some enemy had struck right into the heart of Kubodin's village. Who could do that? Who could get inside?

"How do you know?"

Kubodin seemed agitated. It was one of the few times Asana had ever seen him so, and he knew why. His friend would feel responsible for this.

"She's not in her hut. And traces of blood were found inside. There was a struggle of some sort. But it's worse than that. I set guards to protect her…"

He did not finish the sentence. Asana could see two possibilities though, and both were bad. The guards had proved traitorous, or they had been killed. He thought he knew which was more likely.

"You've found their bodies?"

"Yes. They were good warriors, but they seem to have been killed quickly."

Asana felt his heart sink. "This is the worst news for our land in a thousand years. It's as bad as the death of the emperor long ago."

Kubodin said nothing, but his gaze was bleak. They both knew that if Shar were dead the shamans would control the land into the future, and nothing would ever wrest that power from their hands.

One of Kubodin's men approached. "Chief?"

"What is it, Namrodin?"

"You asked me to go to Nerchak's hut and bring him here."

"Well?"

"He's not there. The hut was empty. The hearth was cold – no fire had been lit at all last night. And it seemed to me that he never slept there."

There was silence for a moment. Asana's mind raced, and he saw Kubodin finger his brass earring. He was thinking too, but there could only be one conclusion.

Kubodin dropped his hand and straightened. "Good work, Namrodin. That will be all."

The young warrior left, and Asana looked into Kubodin's eyes.

"There can be no doubt. It was him. But why?"

"The why will have to wait. We'll know when we catch him."

Asana did not reply. He thought back to the skills Nerchak had shown coming here. Tracking him would be extremely difficult, if it could be done at all.

They waited in silence. Kubodin had already sent men out to ask if anyone had seen or heard anything, and he had also sent men to look for any kind of trail.

Several warriors approached at different times, but their reports were always the same. No one had heard or seen anything unusual.

A little while later report came back that some strange tracks had been found, but the warrior was not sure.

"What was strange about them?" Kubodin asked.

"Nothing, chief. Except this. They were small as though made by a woman, but they were unusually deep. It was like they had been made on purpose to be obvious, but they only showed here and there."

"Good!" Kubodin said. "That sounds like her. She thinks on her feet, that one. Is someone following them?"

"Yes chief. I came back to report, but others kept going."

The warrior left them, and Asana felt relief flood through him. Like Kubodin, he guessed the tracks had been deliberately left by Shar, and that they were only intermittent indicated she had to be careful not to be seen to do so.

"She's still alive," he said. "Thank the gods, she's still alive."

Kubodin nodded. "For the moment at least, but Nerchak won't be for long. When I find him, he'll lose a foot of height fast." As he spoke he gripped hard the haft of his axe.

Asana felt his own anger rise. Nerchak had been one of them. He had been trusted. He had even fought side by side with them, but all along he was working for someone else. It must be the shamans. Yet if so, why had he abducted her instead of killing her? He would have had ample opportunity well before now to do that. It did not make sense.

Sagadar approached with some of his men, and Asana realized this news would please him. He was not a supporter of Shar, but it seemed much of his clan was so he had been forced into backing her. That could all fall apart swiftly.

"Is it true?" he asked. "Is Shar dead?"

"Not dead," Kubodin told him, "but abducted."

The chief of the Night Walker Clan looked suddenly dubious.

"Have you got proof that she lives?"

Kubodin answered abruptly. "Have you got proof that she's dead?"

That seemed to take the other chief by surprise, and Asana admired what Kubodin had done. He had placed an opponent on the back foot, and showed, once more, that his mind was as razor sharp as the blades of his axe that he always sharpened.

Before anything else could be said another messenger arrived.

"We have news, chief," he said to Kubodin. "We traced some tracks to a corral outside the village where the ponies of the messengers are kept. They were all scattered though."

It started to add up to Asana. Of course Nerchak would head there. Ponies offered him and his captive a swift escape.

Kubodin thanked the messenger. "Let's have a look and see if they've discovered anything else." He studied Sagadar briefly, then invited him along.

They walked together through the village in silence. Asana did not think Kubodin wanted the other chief there, but it was a courtesy. More than that, he wanted to keep a close eye on him. While he was under eye, there was less chance that he might decide his agreement with Shar was no longer binding.

The village was boiling with activity. News had spread fast, and many people seemed confused. They had only just discovered that there was a descendant of the emperor still alive, and that the ancient prophecy might be fulfilled. But just as swiftly she was now taken from them, and it seemed the shamans would rule forever.

They went outside of the village and to the enclosure. A few ponies had been brought back, but a quick glance at the earth told Asana all he needed to know. Pony tracks were everywhere, and that was why they had been dispersed. Their movements hid the trail of the two that carried Nerchak and Shar. It was a smart move, and Asana cursed silently.

Kubodin called a man over. "Has anyone discovered anything yet?"

The man hesitated. "There was blood. Someone had been injured, and given the amount, it was no small injury."

Kubodin nodded. "Keep searching. We'll get out of your way."

They went over to stand beneath the shade of a small oak nearby.

"The dead don't bleed," Kubodin said.

It was true, and Asana took some hope from it. Sagadar remained quiet. How much he could be trusted was nothing more than a guess. He had no liking for Shar, but while she was alive he was not likely to betray her. Yet he would not go to war for her either unless she led the army. And the longer she was away, who could say what shifts in loyalty would occur?

Asana sat down, leaning his back against the tree trunk. For now, there was nothing to do but wait and see what further reports Kubodin's men made.

4. Doubt and Delay

For the next little while, more reports came in. No one had found any tracks that showed where Nerchak and Shar had gone.

Kubodin was becoming frustrated, but he showed little of it. Asana felt it too. There was nothing to do but wait though. However, on this point, Kubodin surprised him.

"Come here," Kubodin called over to one of his men nearby.

"Yes chief?"

"Call the search off. Order all men back here as swiftly as possible, with whatever ponies they've managed to find so far. Most of all, fetch me Radatan the hunter, if he was not killed in the recent battle. If he was, fetch me one of his brothers. Quickly!"

Sagadar looked at his fellow chief quizzically. "What's this about, then?"

"Simple," Kubodin replied. "Shar's out there somewhere, all we need to do is track her. But the tracks have been obscured. I can track. And so can many of the men here, but we're not good enough. The hunter I called for is. What might take us days to find, he'll find swiftly. I'd bet on it."

Asana remembered his brief meeting with the hunter. He also remembered that he had worked for Kubodin's father. The skill was there, but how much better he was than these other men remained to be seen. Yet Kubodin would not have called for him unless he truly believed he could do what was required, and fast.

"Still no reason to call off the search," Sagadar said, "until your man arrives. Are you sure you really want to find Shar?"

Asana saw Sagadar pale a little, and looking over at Kubodin he saw why. The little man had an ice-cold look in his eyes, and his hand fondled the hilt of his axe.

"She's the emperor-to-be. You don't know her like I do yet, but when you do you'll love her as I do. For her, and for her cause, I'd lay down my life. Speak no more folly!"

Sagadar's men looked tense at that, but Kubodin ignored them. Their chief diffused the tension with a seemingly easy laugh, but unless Asana was mistaken there was a shiver of fear, or surprise, in it too.

"We'll see, Kubodin. We'll see."

They waited in terse silence after that. Kubodin's men returned and rested under a group of trees nearby. A few stragglers came in soon after, and some of them had ponies that they penned up again in the corral.

Asana felt the passage of time keenly. It was slipping through their fingers like blood from a sword wound. If Shar's trail was not found quickly, and Shar herself soon after, it would be just as lethal. The army she was beginning to build would fall apart, and no matter if she escaped after that it would be hard to start again. Who would follow her once she had failed once? Raising a new army would be twice as hard, and the shamans would see to it that her first failure was known across the land.

Radatan was still evidently alive, for he eventually appeared with some of Kubodin's men.

"Good to see you still alive, Radatan," Kubodin greeted him. "How did you fare in the battle?"

"I survived. Hunters are hard to kill, but a few of your brother's warriors got close."

"It was a good fight, hey?"

Radatan grinned at him. "It was. But I'm getting too old for that."

Kubodin shrugged. "A good fight keeps you young. Anyway, I have a job for you that might be more to your liking."

The hunter nodded. "So I hear. You want me to track that young girl?"

"I do. She was taken, against her will, by the other man that you met with me. We think they came here, and the ponies were scattered to hide their trail. I've called off the men so as not to obscure the tracks any further. Do you think you can find them?"

"Sure chief, I can find them."

Kubodin looked at him intently. "You'll be well rewarded if you can. Nothing is more important than this. Nothing. But the man who took her, Nerchak his name is, he's good with trails. Very good."

Radatan raised an eyebrow. "Well, let's see just how good he is. I *liked* that young girl. Heard more about her after we met, but I liked her at first glance."

The hunter said no more after that, merely walking away without saluting his chief. The hill tribes, Asana knew, were like that. And he liked them for it.

He and Kubodin stood in silence, watching as the hunter went to the center of the corral and walked in slow and ever-widening circles. Soon he had left the corral and moved into the trees. No one followed him, but everyone's eyes were on him.

Radatan moved at a leisurely pace, and here and there he knelt down and he moved his arms in a strange way as though visualizing the movement of whatever left the tracks he saw.

The hunter was soon lost from sight. Asana relaxed, leaning back into the tree trunk. Kubodin lay down near him on the ground and seemed to doze. An observer might think them unconcerned, but it was not the case. They were both warriors, and they rested when they could. If a trail were found they would be fresh, and they would pursue it with all possible speed. Nothing was more important than rescuing Shar, and their relaxed attitude now would help them later.

Clouds passed over the sun, and the world darkened. Then the light flashed back, and insects hummed in the distance. It was a peaceful day, and tranquility infused the air. It would not last though, and at the end of whatever trail they followed would be death. Nerchak would be killed, and all that remained to be seen was if Asana did it himself or Kubodin. Both loved Shar like a daughter. They had never discussed it, but they each knew how the other felt. At first they had helped her because of the prophecy and their dislike of the shamans, but then they had got to know her.

So much hinged on how good a tracker this Radatan was. Kubodin had faith in him though, and that was no small thing. Kubodin was a good tracker himself, and he had not even looked. He must know that the hunter was a lot better, and that was why he had called for him so quickly.

The morning wore on, and then unexpectedly Radatan returned. Unlike before, he now strode swiftly. Kubodin sprang up to meet him, and the rest of the little group, and the warriors nearby, did the same.

"What news?" Kubodin asked.

"I found the trail. Two ponies heading southwest, following a straight line. Only riders do that – ponies by themselves don't. Their tracks were deeper than they should have been too, but most of all it was clear that the first led the second by a rope. It's them, and only them. This Nerchak isn't so good as he thinks."

Kubodin slapped him on the back. "Then we have them!"

The hunter looked at him hesitantly, then spoke. "We have them, but they have a good lead on us, and it'll be slow going following the trail and avoiding any misdirection this Nerchak tried. But…"

"But what?"

"The girl is injured. Perhaps badly. My guess is that she was beaten, and the tracks showed where she staggered a few times. She's in a bad way."

Kubodin nodded. "I guessed as much. Yet if Nerchak wanted her dead, we would have found her body in the hut. This is his way of keeping her compliant while they travel, but there's iron in her. She'll get through it. Just follow her as fast as you can."

Kubodin gave swift orders then. Most men could return to the village, but he, Asana, and a handful of men would follow the trail on ponies. He sent runners back to fetch supplies for them, and then he turned to Sagadar.

"Are you coming?" He had no authority to make it a command, yet the expression on his face made it clear what he expected. It would be an insult to the emperor-to-be if he did not.

"I'll come, with a few of my men."

Asana studied the chief of the Night Walker Clan. He had agreed, and not reluctantly. But he might just as easily hope to find proof of Shar's death, or captivity beyond hope of rescue, in order to satisfy his clan that he had done what he could and then to bring them back under the influence of the shamans.

"Chief!" came a call, and one of Kubodin's men pointed back toward the village. There were men coming, and some rode ponies, but they seemed dressed differently from members of the Two Ravens Clan.

"Who is it?" Asana asked.

It was Sagadar who answered. "I believe they are the chiefs of the Smoking Eyes and Iron Dog Clans. They must have arrived early for Kubodin's ceremony to become chief."

Asana looked them over. They were hard men used to battle and command. Perhaps they had arrived early, but they could hardly have yet received Kubodin's invitation. More likely they had learned of Shar and the other events in this valley from their spies, and they wanted to meet Shar in person, and judge for themselves, and quickly, if they wanted to support her. Coming from the village as they were though, they would have heard of her abduction. It was a bad start to things, and the chances of them giving their support had greatly diminished.

Kubodin went over to greet them. "Hail, chiefs," he said. "I'm Kubodin."

The two chiefs dismounted. One was unusually tall and thin, and his eyes were gray. It was a strange look for someone of Cheng blood, but Asana had heard rumors that other tribes had ventured here on a time from outside the boundaries of the old empire.

The tall man shook Kubodin's hand. "I'm Nahring, chief of the Smoking Eyes Clan."

The other chief took his hand. He was squat and powerfully built, and more in line with the usual types of warriors seen in the hills.

"I'm Dakashul, chief of the Iron Dogs."

They exchanged a few pleasantries fitting for the occasion, but then Kubodin brought the conversation around to the only thing that mattered just now.

"You will have heard that a descendent of the emperor yet lives. Her name is Shar, and I've sworn to serve her. So has Sagadar. But she's been abducted. We go to seek her now, and we go with haste." The little man bowed to the two new chiefs. "If you knew her, as I do, you would be impressed by her. But you don't – so come with me and meet her soon. Make up your own minds."

The Smoking Eyes chief showed nothing of what he thought, and remained silent, but Dakashul scratched his head and answered bluntly.

"It worries me that she was so easily abducted by an enemy. If she can't protect *herself*, how can she protect *us* from the wrath of the shamans? And that will fall on us hard if we even look like following her."

Asana decided to intervene. "I'm no chief," he said, "but my counsels have been known to sway leaders across the land. Will you hear my opinion?"

The newcomers looked at him curiously. "And you might be?" Dakashul asked.

"I go by different names in different lands, but I'm most commonly known as Asana."

The chiefs looked at him intently, and then offered bows after a moment.

"We'd heard you were in the Wahlum Hills," Nahring said. "It's a pleasure to meet you, Asana Gan, and we'll gladly listen to your advice."

Asana held each of their gazes by turn, and he answered softly.

"Make no choices yet. Think neither the good nor the bad. Come with us, for we leave now to bring Shar back. Make up your mind when you meet her. For myself, I'll serve her all the days of my life, and I would die for her. You, who have not met her yet, will think me a fool. But when you meet her, you will change your mind."

The Iron Dog chief scratched the top of his head, then shrugged.

"That sounds fair enough to me. I'm happy to meet her and see."

Nahring gave a more solemn answer. "So will it be, Asana Gan. Your advice is sought out over all the land, and I'm glad to take it."

Kubodin gave some last-minute orders to his men, and he put those in charge that he trusted while he was away. It was a bad time to leave, for he had just secured the chieftainship, and there would yet be those who had served his brother who might try to start trouble. That Kubodin went himself in search of Shar proved his loyalty to her.

They set off. It was a small and mixed company. Asana mused as he rode that there were few places in all the lands of the Cheng where four chiefs might come together as they did here in peace. Even so, each had a small guard of picked warriors, mostly on foot, and there was a certain tenseness. No one expected trouble, but they were ready for it if it broke out.

Much of the morning had passed them by, but the sun was high and bright, and Radatan led them all. He moved fast at first, taking them to the last point where he had followed the tracks to. After that, it was slow going.

The hunter had a pony, and often he leaned over in the saddle, peering at the ground. Sometimes he dismounted and knelt down for a closer inspection of something few others could even see. In him, Asana soon realized, Kubodin had found a good man. He showed none of the stress that might be expected, for the life of the emperor-to-be was in his hands, but he went about his task with swift efficiency.

They followed the trail for the rest of the day, and Radatan pointed out the spots to them where their quarry had dismounted and rested, or eaten a meal. He confirmed Shar was still alive, but he also said there was fresh blood, either from an old injury that had opened or from a new one inflicted on her as they traveled.

When evening came, no one wanted to stop. But not even a tracker of Radatan's skill could follow a trail in the dark.

5. Lord of the Ahat

Nerchak carried on through the night, leading Shar away from the place she had to be, and every step of their ponies was like the erasure of her destiny. The prophecy was dying, and she would die with it.

She rode in a daze, her mind fogged by pain, hunger and a sense of hopelessness. She could no longer fight it, and perhaps it was better not to.

The thought of giving up was anathema to her, and she would never do that. Yet to endure the hardship she was going through, she had to let herself fall into that fog and be swallowed by the numbness. When her opportunity came to escape though, she must flare to life like a fire. And she would. She would give all of herself to that moment, and everything in the meantime was unimportant.

A wolf howled in the distance, and a moment later a dog barked, closer to hand. There was obviously a village nearby, and instantly Nerchak swerved away from the direction of the barking.

It was not long after that he drew to a halt and dismounted. It was not dawn yet, so he would not be establishing a camp. It was merely a rest, and one of the few he had allowed all night.

Shar dismounted at his gesture to do so, and for once he did not strike her. Pain still flared through her though, and she did not sit down as he had but walked on the spot and shrugged her shoulders to try to get the blood flowing properly again, and to loosen the muscles that had begun to cramp up.

Nerchak watched her closely, sipping at his waterbag, and she could see the glint of his eyes in the starlight. Or maybe she was imagining that. Certainly she could see the outline of his face, but her vision was getting blurry. Her eyes were dry from lack of water to drink, and she wondered if her mind was starting to slip and she was beginning to hallucinate.

"Sit down," he ordered. "You're annoying me."

She did as requested. It was not so easy with her arms tied behind her back, and she stumbled. Instantly the glint of steel showed in his hand. He was ready for her to attack him, but he relaxed as he saw that it was just clumsiness on her part.

He looked at her thoughtfully, and this time she was close enough that she really was seeing his face.

"You need some water," he said at length, and handed her the waterbag.

She unstoppered it and tried to drink, but it was empty. At this, Nerchak burst into laughter.

"I guess you'll have to wait until we find a stream, princess."

She let the empty waterbag fall, and looked back at him with the best smile she could manage. Her mouth was dry, and she thought it might have looked like a grimace, but however it looked she was not going to show the rage that flared to life inside her. Best to keep that secret for a little while longer. He would make his first, and last, mistake soon.

He picked up the waterbag and ordered her to mount. The rest break was over. She did so, as always, with his assistance. It was no easy task with her hands tied behind her back, and then they moved ahead into the dark of the grasslands.

Shar took some satisfaction in what she had done. He would try all the harder to break her, having failed to get the reaction he wanted to the empty waterbag.

She mused on that. It was a new tactic to try to break her down. That meant that he realized the old tactics were not working. In turn, that meant he realized she was putting on an act of meekness to lull him into false confidence. Or it was just pure malice. Either way, she would still kill him. That she vowed to herself. One way or another, he would die.

The dark of the grasslands swallowed them up. Under the hooves of the ponies wild sage was crushed, and the scent drifted to Shar. She loved the smell. There were patches of it in Tsarin Fen, but not much. As she had traveled though she realized it was abundant in many places, especially the open plains, and it reminded her of collecting herbs with her grandmother.

At length, the dark sky of the east paled and the light of the stars dimmed as gray washed the heavens. The dawn came, suddenly bright and swift with the rising sun, and a chorus of birdsong greeted it as though welcoming an old friend.

Nerchak pulled Shar down from the horse, causing her to fall badly. But she righted herself and sat. Surely he would give her food and water now. The last part of their journey had been a blur, but she did remember him stopping at a small stream to refill the waterbag.

Whatever he was going to do, he was in no hurry. They were in the open now, and he slowly walked around their camp gazing out carefully in all directions. She knew what he was looking for. Smoke. If there were some, it would indicate a village nearby. Or possibly pursuit if it came from their backtrail. But there was none.

Satisfied, he gathered what dry timber he could from a dead bush nearby. He felt secure enough to light his own fire.

She was allowed to drink, and even given a little food. Nerchak did not strike or belittle her either. Nevertheless, she knew this was just part of his strategy to break her. He would offer punishment and reward by turns in order to make her dependent on him. It would not work, but he did not know that, and in the meantime she could make use of this change to further her own knowledge of the situation.

"You're not taking me to Three Moon Mountain. So who are the dark forces you mentioned?"

He looked at her for a moment, then shrugged. "Why not? I may as well tell you a little. You'll find out soon enough anyway, and it might make you realize how impossible your situation is."

The fire was burning low, and the dry timber had not smoked much, so he put a few more branches on the red coals.

"My people, the Ahat, were sent to kill Shulu Gan. It was discovered where she was in Tsarin Fen, but she has escaped such situations before. This time though, there was time to plan an effective strike with multiple assassins all at once. Even so, because of the ample time we had to plan, a second force was sent. Its purpose was to establish a ring around Tsarin Fen so that even if she escaped the first strike the second would take her."

Shar looked away at that. She had given much thought to the perils she faced herself, but not enough to her grandmother.

"I see that disturbs you. My advice is to accept it and get on with the rest of your own life, however short that may be. Shulu is dead now. She could not have escaped. Not this time."

Shar turned back to hold his gaze. "I don't think so. Shulu is too wily to be caught. She's like one of the fen wolves – you might hear one but sightings are rare. And if pressed into a corner, she has claws and fangs."

"Your adulation of her is misplaced. She's old now. Ancient. Her power has waned. If she's not dead yet, she soon will be."

Shar grinned at him. He was always trying to influence her mind, but she could play that game too.

"You might be right. Her power isn't what it was. Even so, I don't think she's dead. More likely she's out there somewhere," and Shar gestured vaguely with her head, "planning and plotting a way to help me. I'm sure of it."

He did not like that. He did not like it at all. "No. She's dead. At the least, she's abandoned you. She could have fled Tsarin Fen with you, but she didn't. And her waning magic isn't enough to protect her. The Ahat don't fear magic anyway. It's no defense against a knife in the back."

Shar decided to let the subject drop. She knew what she knew, but there were other things to discuss while Nerchak was in the mood for talking.

"You said the Ahat were sent to kill Shulu. What of me?"

He hesitated, seemingly debating what he should tell her.

"You were different. You're wanted alive, at least for now. Only some of the Ahat sent to your village even knew about you. There were different missions. It was the same with the ring set up around the fen as well. Some had orders to kill Shulu. Some had orders to capture you. But *I* was the who did it, and my standing will rise high because of it."

Shar did not doubt it. She was a prize, at least to the shamans. But she needed to know more of these mysterious powers that worked behind even them.

"Who gave these orders? If the shamans didn't employ the Ahat, who did?"

This time, he nearly did not answer. But well trained as he was for someone so young, the fault of pride still got the better of him.

"The Ahat accept many tasks. We are blades in the dark for hire, but out Great Master is above that. The shamans think they control him, but he controls them instead. He knows their secrets. He chooses who among them lives or dies. They fight among each other, always seeking to pull down those above them so that they might rise themselves. The Great Master accepts some requests for assassination, and refuses others. Those he advances owe him. Those he warns and saves, they owe him too. His is the true power in the land, and he uses it more ruthlessly than the shamans use theirs."

Shar considered all that. She could not be sure if he were lying or telling the truth. Yet it did have the ring of truth to it. If so, he had made an error. Knowledge was power, and she must find a way to use what he had given her. It had been given out of pride, or maybe spite to make her fear her future even more, but either way she would use it.

"Who is this Great Master that leads the Ahat?"

"Enough," he said. "I've told you more than I should have already. Who he is you'll discover when you meet him. If it pleases him to talk to you rather than slit your throat himself."

He had revealed more, and Shar began to get a sense that he was overconfident now. He had been tasked with capturing her, but for what purpose he had no idea. Nor did she know what this Great Master intended, but as she thought on him she remembered the vision she had been given by the seer in the mountains before she found the Swords of Dawn and Dusk. In particular, she remembered the old man who she did not know but felt was her implacable enemy.

An idea occurred to her, and she did not know if her guess was right, but she would put it to the test. Nerchak liked to play games with her mind, but she could do the same to him. She could fill his thoughts with doubt, and that might lessen his vigilant watch over her. It was all she could do, for the moment.

"I think you underestimate Shulu. She *knows* who your mysterious leader is. He's an old man, hooded and cloaked. He hides his face, but when you catch a glimpse of it you think he's kindly. But a closer look shows that there's something very, very wrong about him."

Shar saw the shock on Nerchak's face, and knew her guess had been right and her attack had struck its mark. She drove it home further.

"He's a dead man. He just doesn't know it yet. The only question is whether he'll die before, or after, you."

Nerchak had not regained his composure, and he answered almost as if to himself.

"No one knows what he looks like. *No one.* Few even of the Ahat do."

Shar looked as nonchalant as she could. "Yet I just described him. I told you that you underestimated Shulu. She *will* kill him."

Her captor seemed to regain himself, and he realized that he had told her too much and allowed her to plant a seed of doubt in his mind. He rose and kicked her in the head. She was expecting it, and leaned back to absorb the blow. Even so, she was not sure that he had not broken her jaw.

He tied her legs together harshly with some rope, for there was no tree nearby to secure her against, and moved to the other side of the camp to lay down and rest.

Shar rested too, and despite her pain, and blood from the blow trickling down her face until she tasted it in her mouth, she smiled.

Her tactic to unnerve him had worked. Yet at the same time, she had undermined her strategy of lulling him to believe she felt beaten.

6. Act of War

Asana was not a skilled rider, but he liked his shaggy pony and he found that riding freed the mind to think.

He held back from the lead group. There the chiefs rode with Kubodin, and they huddled around him talking closely. Why had they come?

It was not for Shar, and that was a problem. No doubt they were interested in her. She had come to the Wahlum Hills like a storm and blown through them, touching every tree and shifting every branch. Destiny came with her, and the prophecy was on everyone's lips. Yet all storms pass and are forgotten, or mostly forgotten, and her abduction had robbed her of momentum. It had undermined her and sapped away the magic of who she was.

The situation could be remedied, but every day that went by made it harder. A certain curiosity drove the chiefs to meet the descendant of Chen Fei, but that was not enough. They might rescue her, but having done so, would they then commit to following one they themselves had saved?

Curiosity had driven them here, but it was not the only reason they came. Nor was it why they had come early. Kubodin was a new chief, and there were alliances to make, agreements of trade to renegotiate, and no doubt he would also receive offers of marriage to tie him close to them. They sought advantage against the other tribes, and that they were alone with Kubodin without competition was a boon to them.

Kubodin would know all this though, but it was secondary to him. His first responsibility was to Shar, and to the empire that could be. He would stall them. He would lead them tentatively forward but commit to nothing until they had found Shar, and the chiefs had a chance to be impressed by her.

The small party moved down a slope, thick with trees. It seemed there had been many slopes of late, most going downward. The Wahlum Hills were coming to an end, but how far out beyond them the chiefs of the hill tribes were willing to go, if at all, was a question yet to be answered.

As always, Radatan led them. Presently, he dismounted and led his horse by hand while studying the trail. It was one of the few places where it was obvious, and Asana wondered why he did so. Then he realized. If Nerchak had attempted to misdirect them by laying down a false trail, this was the sort of place he would use to do it and he would deliberately make sure it was easy to discover.

Radatan was up to the challenge. Halfway down the slope he called a halt and scouted out to the east by himself. He disappeared well into the trees, but his voice drifted to them as though from far away.

"This way!" the hunter called, and the party obediently turned and went in the new direction.

Asana went back to thinking about the chiefs. He was sure they were tired of the dominance of the shamans. A chief was supposed to be the focus of the clan's power, and to rule the people with justice and for their benefit. Yet over the centuries, bit by bit, the shamans had usurped their power. Nearly all decisions were jointly made now by the chief, a council of elders, and the shamans. Given that the shamans also helped choose the council members, theirs was the will that held sway.

The chiefs resented that erosion of their power. That much Asana knew. It was also an erosion of the power of the people, for the chiefs represented them and could be replaced if they did not serve their people well. Yet what good was that when the next chief would only be weaker against the established shaman and council?

Asana was sure the chiefs were interested in Shar. She offered hope of another way, but right now she appeared weak. It would be hard for a chief to side with her because he would wonder if the shamans would win in the end, and in doing so all those who supported Shar, simple warrior or chief alike, would be killed. So not only might they refuse to support her, it was possible if they rescued her they might decide to hand her over to the shamans themselves.

The group passed through a rocky gully now, mostly bare of trees, and came to a glade at the end of it amid a small wood. Here Radatan pointed out an old campsite.

"The coals are cold," he said. "For all that this Nerchak is taking time to try to hide his trail, he's still moving fast."

"Are we gaining on him?" Kubodin asked.

"A little only. But that's not the worst of it."

"What is, then?"

"There's more blood. By the signs of it, he's beating the girl hard. And repeatedly."

Kubodin looked cold as the starless void. "Then we had best hurry."

Radatan led them quickly then, but only a little more so than he had been doing. If he were fooled by some deception in the trail, that would slow them far more and could not be afforded. The man's skill was truly great though, and Asana was impressed.

The mood of the travelers was subdued. Whatever the chiefs, and their retinues, thought of Shar, they did not like to see a woman beaten. If they caught up with Nerchak it would go very badly for him, but that was a separate issue to whether or not they would recognize her as emperor.

Asana nudged his shaggy pony forward to catch up to the lead group.

"You have a good man there," he said to Kubodin.

"He served my father well, but he's serving me even better."

They rode in silence for a little while after that. In the distance they heard drums briefly, then they faded away. The little group of riders had been seen, but Asana was not sure by whom. This was no longer Two Ravens land, nor that of the other chiefs. Yet their group was large enough, and esteemed enough with several chiefs, that there would be no trouble. They would be watched closely though, but as long as they did no damage they would not be taken for a raiding party.

"You've traveled across the lands of the Cheng lately?" It was Nahring who asked the question, and he looked at Asana with those steady gray eyes that were like those of the people of the faraway lands of Alithoras that Asana had recently come from.

"I have. At least, this eastern portion. To the west, I haven't been in a long while."

"What news is there?"

"The same as always. Tribes mistrust tribes. There is great poverty. Sickness and hunger are not uncommon. The triseptium year hasn't changed that."

The other man looked grim. "It's the same here. We have had a better year than many, for the rains were good last year and our crops of grain flourished. Whatever store we build though doesn't last long into a bad year."

Asana wondered where this was going, but he felt it was no idle conversation. The chief was asking him this for a reason.

"Is it true that you have lived for a long while outside our lands?"

"I have, and Kubodin with me. Most recently we were in one of the great cities of the eastern people. Faladir it's called."

"I've heard of it," Nahring said. "How are those people organized? Is it true that they have kingdoms?"

Asana understood the purpose of these questions now. Nahring was thinking of Shar, and how best to run a land. He was wondering if an empire was better for the people than scattered tribes.

"They have kingdoms. None, by themselves, are as vast as the lands of the Cheng, but they're still large. One king rules each kingdom, and their power is great. Yet they are advised by wise men of the realm, and the rights of the people are established by tradition. A king who transgresses against that is at risk of being deposed."

Asana thought quickly on what he would say next. He wanted to help Shar, but likewise he would not lie.

"None of that is to say that things are perfect in those realms. Overall, they are richer than us, and live better lives. They have no tribal wars. All of the land works together as one, and the power of the state protects each and every member. Wars between kingdoms are rare. Mostly, they work together against their common enemies from the lands to the south and north. They're a free people, strong and proud. But I say again, they aren't perfect."

Nahring guided his pony around a fallen tree. "And what of shamans? Do they not have any?"

"They don't. They have what they call lòhrens, what we would call a sage or a wizard."

"What powers do they have?"

"They have great power. Enormous. They don't govern in any sense though. They help protect the people if they are attacked, and they defend against sorcery.

They're wise, and they offer advice when it's sought, but they rule nowhere and they rule nothing."

Nahring asked no more. Asana knew he had given him something to think about, and it truly was. The lands of the east were remarkably free by Cheng standards, and it could be the same here if the grip of the shamans was broken.

They moved at a fast pace, seldom resting for time was precious. The chiefs withstood it well. Kubodin was used to it, but the others could not have been. They rarely traveled outside their own small chiefdoms. Even so, they made no complaint nor asked for a rest. The warriors of the hills, even their chiefs, were tough. They would make the foundation of a fine army for Shar, if only she were free to lead them and to gather more tribes to her.

The afternoon wore on, and Asana wondered what would happen when they came to the end of the Wahlum Hills. If they had not rescued Shar by then, would the chiefs continue? Without doubt, Kubodin would. That would make two of them. Of the others though, it was hard to say. Likely, they would not venture outside their own territory. Few among the Cheng ever did, shamans, nazram and traders aside.

As the long shadows of dusk lengthened, reaching back toward the lands they had come from to meet the mists that rolled down from the higher hills, the party came to a bluff. From here, they could see a sunlit plain extend out to the west, and afar the marching Eagle Claw Mountains.

Somewhere below Shar was held captive. There was no sign of any movement out there, but she was close.

They could go no farther today. The sun set swiftly, and a camp must be prepared. Kubodin requested that no fires be lit. It would reveal to Nerchak that he was pursued, and that could cause him to kill Shar.

The other chiefs agreed, and a cold meal was prepared for all of them, of which Asana partook as their guest. Most chiefs throughout the land gave him such honors. Being a famous *gan* had its rewards.

Kubodin sipped a little wine from a simple wooden cup.

"Radatan thinks that by this time tomorrow we'll catch up with them."

There it was, Asana thought. Kubodin had been thinking exactly what he himself had been. Would the chiefs leave their own land? This was his subtle way of broaching the subject, but also, in a way that was not assertive, merely revealing his expectation that they would do so.

"By tomorrow," Sagadar replied, "we'll be out on the grasslands and in the tribal grounds of the Green Hornet Clan. Are we going to risk that?"

"I'll risk it, for Shar," Kubodin said.

"As will I," Asana added instantly.

In the gathering gloom Asana could still see doubt on the faces of the others though.

Dakashul voiced it. "It would be folly. To go out there would be an act of war against the Green Hornets. It would invite them to start raiding into the hills."

"I had not thought," Kubodin replied, "that an Iron Dog would ever give up a quest once begun."

The other man did not look happy. "I don't like it, but we each have our clans to think about. If the hills are raided, people will die, and not just warriors. Cattle will be stolen, villages burned. Is that what you want?"

"No," Kubodin said simply. "But I'll not abandon the emperor-to-be. Nor a friend in need."

They gave no answer to that. Both sides of the problem had been clearly put, and there were no easy answers.

Asana knew where Dakashul was coming from, and he guessed Sagadar would be of the identical view.

"What of you, Nahring?" he asked. "You've given no opinion."

The chief of the Smoking Eyes Tribe looked out into the gathering night.

"Going into Green Hornet lands could start a war. Nor are we a large enough party to defend ourselves if they attack us in force. The risks are high, but likewise the risk of losing a descendant of Chen Fei is unthinkable."

It was not quite an answer, but it was clear there would be none tonight. They put off a decision until the morning, and talked instead of many things as the night darkened about them.

They were growing tired, but Kubodin called for a story.

"You know much of the land and its history, Asana," he said "and you're a good teller of tales. Tell us something now to ease our hearts."

Asana took a sip of wine. This was no idle request, but Kubodin being subtle. He wanted to persuade the chiefs to not give up on Shar, and yet to do it in a way where no one could be seen to be trying to talk them into anything.

"Very well," he answered, looking at Kubodin in the dark. "I know just the story for this moment."

No one else spoke. Among the Cheng, storytelling was popular. It was a way that they honored the ancestors of the past, and it was especially liked in the rural communities such as this.

"On a time," Asana began, "the emperor was a youth. He had not yet gathered armies to him, nor did he rule. He was growing into his manhood, and he worked as a woodcutter. He learned the skill from his father, though it was said his heart rather yearned for the farming life that his mother had been brought up in. Even so, because of the strength of his arm and his skill with an axe, he was good at what he did."

Asana took another sip of his wine. This was a story that was well known across the land, but he had found that people loved to hear it, and he had acquired a depth of facts for it from reading the old histories that few other people, except the shamans, knew.

"One morning when the world was younger than it is now, and fairer and brighter, he worked with a team of men from his village felling trees on a ridge nearby. Yet though the world was better than it is now, yet still there was crime and sorrow. A call went up from one of the men who had dropped his axe and pointed. *Fire*, the woodcutter cried.

"Chen Fei followed with his eyes where the man indicated. A great curl of smoke was billowing up from the village. It could have been a bonfire to destroy rubbish, but he knew it was not.

"Bandits had come. It was rumored that other villages had been raided in the lands about, but none near where he lived.

"The woodcutters gathered up their axes and ran toward their home. Yet Chen was faster. Like a leaping deer he sprang away, and though the slope was steep he dared to run it at full speed. Somehow, he survived, for to fall was to risk breaking his neck on the uneven ground.

"He outstripped the others, being both faster and more daring. For he also ran straight into a wood where an ambush might be set. The others took a longer way home that kept them on open ground.

"Chen knew the risks of what he did. Yet his mother and father lived in the village, and he loved them dearly. It was known that bandits acted so, setting up a separate trap for men working away from their villages when they saw the smoke. It was especially so for smaller villages like his.

For larger ones, the bandits raided and then fled before the men returned from the fields.

"He knew the risks, and he took them, for ever his heart was full of love and courage both. But the risks were great, and he was by himself. Nor did destiny favor him that day.

"Chen raced ahead, leaping a fallen log, and he came to the center of a clearing. There ten warriors, fierce and thirsty for blood, came out of the trees ahead and surrounded him."

Asana paused. From the circle of men nearby where the retinues of the chiefs had gathered, laughter broke out. They were telling their own stories, but the chiefs near him were intent on him alone.

"It was a dangerous moment," Asana continued. "He who would become the emperor of the Cheng lands could have died. Yet the story tells that his mind was clear, and that no danger ever upset him. Life, death, happiness or sorrow were always said to recede from his mind in the great moments, and all that was left was his heart of courage.

"The bandits ringed him, and their leader called out demanding he cast down his weapon and hand over whatever money he had. Either that, or die.

"In truth, he was a poor man from a poor village. He had little in the way of coin, but he answered them from the proudness of his heart. He told them it was *his* money, and he had earned it with the sweat of his body. If they wished it, they must earn it with their blood.

"The bandits attacked. Chen should have died, for he had not been trained as a warrior and he was far outnumbered. So too, the stories tell, he was a gentle person and disliked violence, preferring instead the tranquility of nature and contests of the mind.

"Chen defended himself with his axe, and he was strong and skilled. A man fell before him, cleft through the head, yet before his body touched the ground another man was slain, his backbone broken and blood spurting from his body.

"The warriors paused then in surprise, but Chen did not. He leaped among them, taking advantage of their startlement, and his axe rose and fell harvesting a gruesome toll among the forest of his enemies."

Asana sipped more wine. There were commentaries in some of the books he had read about this story. They claimed that it was an exaggerated account. That might have been so, but those commentators had not fought for their lives as Chen had on that day. They did not know what it was like to have the spirit of a warrior burn in their bodies like flame in a lamp. Once unleashed, it could consume all before it.

"It is said that Chen swept among them, killing them all. At the last, one man tuned to flee seeing all his brethren killed, but the axe smote him down and Chen leaped over his body as he raced on to his village.

"Waylaid as he had been, yet still he arrived home before the other woodcutters, and there he found great devastation. Murder had been done, and theft and arson. Half the village was destroyed, and a third killed. His parents lived though, and he went to them. There he vowed to learn how to fight better, and how to better protect the village.

"When it was discovered what he had done, and the courage that was in him, and after he had rebuked the village chief for failing to protect the people, the people in turn raised him up to be their leader. So was his long journey to emperor begun."

The chiefs around him stirred, but Asana was not quite done.

"That was the kind of man the emperor was. He had a simple spirit of gentleness, and yet when provoked he would unleash hell upon his enemies. You will find, my friends, as Kubodin already knows, that Shar is the same. You will see."

Kubodin nodded grimly, his face obscure in the dark but Asana could almost feel the determination radiating off him. He agreed, but whether or not the chiefs would be with him was another matter.

They set guards for the night, who would rotate in shifts. Radatan was excused from this because he was fully utilized already during the day, but he insisted on taking a turn anyway. So did Asana, and he reminded them all that Nerchak was skilled and bold. It was not beyond him to come into the camp and kill them all in their sleep if they were lax.

Asana took his turn around the middle of the night. It grew cool. And the fog remained heavy on the higher hills but did not come down to their camp. He sat on an old stump and gazed out over the vast gulf of blackness where the grasslands lay. Shar was there somewhere, and he wished she knew that her friends were coming to help her.

He took out the small statue that Shulu Gan had given him. It was her likeness, and he remembered their meeting, and after his first meeting with Shar.

The statue felt warm to the touch, and he wondered what it was in truth. Certainly, there was magic in it. But of what kind? What purpose did it serve?

It was still on his mind later when he went to sleep again, but he woke to a bright dawn and forgot about it. He also woke to the sound of voices. The chiefs were debating whether or not to go ahead, and the phrase *act of war* was repeated several times.

A new voice broke out, and it was loud and crisp. Nor was it one of the chiefs.

"Look!" Radatan commanded.

There was silence as everyone gazed in the direction that he was pointing.

Asana saw instantly what the hunter meant. Below them, leaving the grasslands and trotting up the hill, came two riders. Who they were, or what they wanted, no one could say. But Asana's hand felt the statue by accident in his pocket, and it seemed not just warm to touch now but hot.

7. You're Dead

Night enveloped the grasslands, but even as the sun began to drop Nerchak started their trek again, and Shar, by force, followed.

She gazed at his back as the ponies walked ahead, and if her hatred were a physical thing, it would have drilled a hole through him. But it was not, and hatred did not serve her now. Patience was her friend.

She thought as they rode. Shulu had not taught her much of this place, but it would be best to recall what she had learned. The tribe that lived here was small, and they called themselves the Green Hornets. At first, she could not remember why that was, and it annoyed her. She knew the names of all the clans throughout the old empire of the Cheng, and their traits. Shulu had insisted on it, and for good reason. Only by such intimate knowledge could she hope to form alliances, or conquer, or win clans to friendship.

It came to her then. This was a small tribe, and they were not greatly skilled in conventional battle. Yet they had deep skill with poisons, and they used venomed arrows and darts that could kill even when the wound was not fatal.

She wondered if Nerchak knew that. The Ahat were said themselves to have the greatest knowledge of poisons, and it occurred to her that maybe the Ahat were a part of the Green Hornet Tribe. No one knew the homeland of the Ahat, so it might as well be here. Yet he did not look like he was doing more than passing through these lands. He showed no signs of stopping or veering from the path that would take them to the next tribe. That was the Soaring Eagles, whom she knew better than other tribes. And they were said to have an ongoing feud with the Green Hornets. Likely, when they got to the borderlands between the tribes, there would be a high number of scouts on patrol. Whether that would be a good thing or not for her, she could not decide.

Nerchak slowed. Ahead, in the gloom, some lights twinkled. Most likely it was a village, and once more they began the long task of circling around it. As they did so, the wind came from a different direction, and the scent of smoke was on it.

They soon came to a depression, ringed by shrubs, and here Nerchak halted for a rest. Unusually, he built a fire. Shar was surprised by that because they were still close to the village, but it made sense in a way. His fire could not be seen, and the scent of it on the air would mingle with that from the village. Should anyone happen to be nearby and smell it, they would assume it came from there.

Nerchak prepared a meal, and he ate it with great relish. He gave no food to Shar, and she began to feel weak with hunger. He did give her a little water though, and she squatted by the fire, enjoying the warmth from it.

When he was done with the meal he kneeled down beside her. She thought that he was about to check the rope that tied her hands behind her back once more, and then start to ride again. But he did not. Instead, he placed a hand against her thigh.

His touch revolted her. "Go ahead," she said with all the disdain she could muster. "I'm going to kill you anyway. Give me a reason to make it a long and painful death."

His face twisted into a snarl, and he punched her square in the head. Yet this was the moment she had long waited for, and endured hell to reach. He had made a mistake at last, and she had anticipated the blow.

She rocked her head back to take away much of the force, and in the same motion gathered her legs under her and propelled herself at him, side on.

Nerchak tried to move back, but she had not been knocked down to the ground as he had expected. His reaction was slow, and she hit him with her full weight.

Her attack was nothing though. Tied as she was, he could easily repel her, yet she was not counting on strength to aid her. The hilt of one of her swords dug deep into his flesh, and he screamed. The magic in them flared to life, and he knew it and knew how he had been baited into a rash response. He tried desperately to scramble away, but her weight was upon him, and the magic flashed forth.

None but the heir to the emperor could touch those swords, the legends claimed. And Shulu had told her it was so. Should any try, the magic in them would be unleashed, and death would result.

She smelled burnt flesh over the smoke in the air, and Nerchak screamed again. He used his strength and threw her off. The magic had harmed him, but not had time to kill him.

Yet she was ready for that, too. All her life she had trained against those who were bigger and stronger. Even as she was propelled off him she came to her feet and lashed out with a kick. She put all the force into it that she could, for if she failed now she would be given no opportunity to escape in the future.

Nerchak was coming to his feet, but one hand was still on the ground for balance. Her blow slipped past his other hand trying to block it, and it crashed into his head. There was a sickening thud, but it seemed satisfying to Shar, and her opponent dropped down to the ground.

She kicked again, this time more of a stomp, but he did not move. Almost, she kicked him once more. The rage inside her that had been pent up had found a release, and she stood over him like the shadow of death.

Trembling, she heaved for breath. The pain from when he had punched her blossomed onto her consciousness, but she ignored it. Reason returned, and she thought with cold logic. The next step was to sever her bonds. Only then was she free.

She knelt down beside him, knowing it was all over for her if he was feigning being knocked out, and reached for his knife. It was awkward with her hands behind her back, but she drew it from its sheath in his belt, and then staggered away.

Still he did not move, and she worked swiftly but with difficulty to saw through the bonds. He began to groan, and she stepped in and kicked him once more in the head.

At last the rope was severed, and her shaking hands were free.

"Yes!" she cried, and she cared not if her voice carried to someone in the wild. She was *free*, and now she was a match for anything.

Her hands ached as the circulation returned, and she wondered if any permanent damage had been done. Quickly though, she rolled Nerchak over and used that same rope to tie his own hands together behind his back. She was none too gentle, and she did not care. Quickly she searched his saddlebags and found another length of rope. With this, she bound his feet together.

She drew his sword and cast it aside. She found another knife up his sleeve, and yet another one strapped to his left leg underneath his trousers. They were all discarded well away from him.

At last she was satisfied. She was free, and he was no longer a threat. He lay there, unmoving, blood seeping from an unseen wound beneath his hair, and she repressed the urge to kill him. She was surprised how strong it was, but it passed. She had a use for him yet, and then he would die. She kept her promises.

She went to his pony and drank deeply from the waterbag. She wanted to clean her face from the dirt and dried blood that caked it, but there was not enough left for that, and she had to be careful to make what was left last.

When her thirst was quenched, she tied the waterbag back up and leaned against the pony. From out of nowhere tears welled to her eyes, and she wept. She could not stop, and her body shook with the effort. It was a strange feeling, for she rarely cried. Yet it felt good to her, and when she was done it was as though she could look at the world differently.

She was alive. She had overcome her captor. What was needed now was to return to the Wahlum Hills and take up again the reigns of her army, if any were still willing to follow her.

Speed mattered now, for the longer she was away the worse it would be. She led the ponies over to Nerchak, and noticed that he was stirring. Her raging desire to kill him assaulted her again, but it passed once more.

"You'll use the pony you had me on," she said. "I'll help you up, but if you try anything I'll kill you. Do you understand."

He nodded, but she was not sure that he did. He still seemed like a drunk man. Head blows could do that. Or it might be a trick.

She helped him up, and he leaned against the pony. She grabbed hold of him and heaved, and managed to get him over the saddle like a sack of grain. Had it been a taller horse, she could not have done so.

Quicky she tied him, and she thought nothing of his discomfort. This was exactly what he had done to her, and it was what he deserved. Justice was sweet.

The ponies were still tied together, and she led them away from the clearing and back toward the hills. She took a last look at the camp. Her life had changed here. Whether it was destiny, blind luck, or her own strength and courage did not seem to matter. All were one in the end.

"Enjoy the ride," she said, but Nerchak did not answer. He may have fainted again, but she did not care.

She set a swift pace. It was not entirely safe in the dark, for a horse could break a leg in an unseen hollow, but she risked it. She had to get back to the hills swiftly.

After a few hours Nerchak began to moan, and she knew the ropes were cutting into him and his position on the horse was probably hurting him too. She kept going.

"I'll kill you!" he began to scream, over and again.

Shar did not answer, but dismounted. First she checked the ponies over, ensuring they were holding up to the effort and giving them a rest and pat down. The second pony was still a little lame, but it had not gotten worse. It might though, with Nerchak's extra weight.

When she was done, she checked the ropes that bound her captive, and then drew a knife and pressed it against the side of his neck.

"You're dead now, snake. I'm taking you back to the hill tribes for questioning. I believe most tribes have a habit of torturing and killing Ahat whenever they're caught, but if you keep yelling out I'll slit your throat and be done with it. Do you understand?"

He did not answer. She resisted the temptation to strike him as he had done to her. His silence was all she wanted, and she had got that.

She mounted and rode on. Time passed, and Nerchak made no further sound. He had believed her threat, and so he should have because it was no bluff.

After that, travel became a blur. She rode, rested, checked his bindings, and rode again. She lit no fires, and rested every few hours but never for long. Time pressed, and she felt a great urgency to return to her army.

Her army might be lost to her though. On Kubodin and Asana she could count, but the rest might fall back to their old ways and accept the rule of the shamans without her. Not only that, but the other hill tribes that had not yet come to join her might never do so now. And she needed them.

The force she could build here was as nothing compared to the mighty armies the shamans could raise from all over the land. Without doubt, they were already moving against her in some way. The time she had lost was precious, and could never be regained.

She would try though. She knew what these warrior chiefs were like, and she knew she had fallen in their eyes. Yet if she returned to them, not just overcoming her captor but bringing him back as a captive in turn, it might win some respect from them. All the more so when they discovered he was an Ahat.

Night faded to dawn, and the hills were ahead of her, wreathed in mist. She did not stop, but began the climb as morning woke the sleeping world in glory. The hills were a wild place, primitive and remote. If she had time, she would love to explore them. She had no time though. She had no purpose other than to build an army and depose the shamans. After that, she dared not let herself think. It was too far away, and the urgent needs of the present too many. They pressed in on her without cessation.

She was tired. She ached all over, yet as she came out of a small wood and turned a little to find the easiest path upward, hope and joy surged through her.

Ahead, looking down from the top of the ridge, was a group of warriors, and she was sure, even from this distance, that she recognized Kubodin and Asana, standing side by side.

They had come for her.

8. Respect

Asana's heart fluttered in his chest as he watched the two ponies climb the slope before him. The chiefs and warriors nearby were deathly silent. Nothing else in the world mattered at that moment. All that counted was who was approaching.

He hoped it was Shar. He *believed* it was Shar, though how he knew he could not be sure. At times, the power of foretelling came over him, but it was rare. Yet perhaps he just imagined it was her because that was what, above all else in the world, he wanted.

The ponies came closer, and the rider on the lead horse rode proud in the saddle. The second rider, he could now see, was tied over the back of the animal. His fists clenched, and around him the tension in the air was alive.

Kubodin was beside him, and the little hill man seemed to tremble. Asana could barely look away from the rider, but he glanced momentarily at the chiefs. They stood still as statues, their gazes fixed.

The lead rider turned their pony a little to the side to follow the path as it wound upward. Long black hair streamed behind her, and Asana's heart missed a beat.

A moment later, the rider straightened toward them again and nudged her pony into a fast trot. It was Shar. It *was* Shar, and Asana felt joy well through him such as he had rarely felt before.

Kubodin voiced his feeling. "Hey ho!" the little man exclaimed, and he threw his arms in the air and danced a jig.

Asana grinned. The other chiefs seemed unsettled, and unsure how to react. He did not blame them. A moment before they had been debating whether or not to venture onto foreign soil to rescue her, and now she returned to them of her own accord.

More than that, she brought a prisoner. It could only be Nerchak. She had freed herself somehow, turning abductor into captive. If that did not sway the chiefs, nothing would.

Shar drew up before them, and now that she was close Asana and those about him could see the terrible trial she had been through. There was blood caked in her hair, and it streaked her face as well. Dirt covered her. Bruises blotched her face, and one eye was nearly swollen shut. Her nose was bloody, and likely broken. Yet somehow she had triumphed, and a grin broke out over her face.

"Thanks for coming, boys. But I have things in order."

Asana's heart swelled in sympathy. She had been through hell such as few could endure and not be broken, yet she smiled at them. Even so, beneath that mask he saw her terrible tiredness, and the shadow of pain that hung over her.

He went forward to help, but somehow ended up bowing to her. When he straightened, he saw that Kubodin had done so as well. All around, the retinues of the chiefs did likewise, and even the chiefs, moved perhaps, or just caught up in the moment, did so too.

He helped her dismount, and up-close saw that her injuries were even worse.

"I'm so pleased to see you, Shar. We've been worried."

She winked at him. "I've been worried about you."

It was an act. He could see it clearly. She had surmised that some of these other men were chiefs, and she was playing her role perfectly to win their respect.

Kubodin came over, and surprisingly he hugged her. Even she seemed surprised by that. All the more so when he picked her up and swung her around in a circle.

She grinned at him when he put her down, and then pointed at the chiefs.

"I haven't come without a gift, but you'll have to share him, I'm afraid."

Sagadar replied. "It is good to see you, lady. Have no fear. Your abductor will be dealt with."

Shar grinned at him. "I have no fear. Don't worry about that. But you'll find that he's more than an abductor."

"How so?"

"Pull up his sleeves, and you'll see."

Sagadar raised his eyebrows at that, but said nothing. They all went over to where Nerchak was slung over the horse and tied. He was conscious, but said nothing.

Asana had a sudden feeling he knew what would happen next, and his glance darted at Shar. She was no longer smiling.

Sagadar pulled up a sleeve, and revealed was the twining snake tattoo.

"An Ahat!"

The others crowded around excitedly and looked.

"You defeated an Ahat?" Sagadar asked.

"I'm not a figurehead, Sagadar," Shar replied. "The blood of the great emperor runs in my veins. I'm the descendant of Chen Fei, and heir to his empire. I have some small skill at fighting. And other things."

They all looked at her then, and beaten and bloody as she was, yet still she stood tall and gave proof to her words. There was a spirit in her that soared above the normal person, and a sense of destiny that wreathed her with greater glory than a golden crown.

One of the chiefs stepped forward. "My name is Nahring, and I lead the Smoking Eyes Clan. I salute you, and I recognize you as emperor-to-be. My clan, and myself, are yours to command."

Dakashul bowed. "I'm chief of the Iron Dogs, and likewise I recognize you. In you rests the hope of the people, and not just my clan."

Asana sensed that destiny charged the very air. Against all hope Shar had returned to them, and she had done so in a way that enhanced her power. Her abduction had served to strengthen her position rather than diminish it, and only fate could unfold like that.

9. The Conclave

Shulu liked the Forest of Dreams. It was a dark place of tall pines that was shadow haunted and magic infused. Here old things lived, more ancient than the magic of the shamans.

Yet it was a place to be careful. There were old magics to be sure, and old enmities that went with them. Not all that dwelled in Alithoras served the Dark, yet not all were friendly to humanity. Or even of humanity.

It was a good place to hide though, and she needed that. Never had she felt so tired. Never so alone. Never so in need of the great strength she had in her youth, that was now fallen like the needles of the pines around her back into the earth. Nature gave, and nature took. The wheel of time ran its race, and it rolled only toward death.

But she was not dead yet. Where strength had once served her, cunning must take its place. Hers was a just cause. And though the shamans outnumbered and outpowered her, did they have the strength of her conviction? Were they willing to die for their cause?

They were a pack of rats, swift to turn on each other and loathsome. They would bully where they could. They would take control where people let them. Yet at the end of the day they had the hearts of cowards.

They could still be dangerous though, and like rats they were cunning. They would kill her if they could, and Shar too. They would destroy all the land merely to rule over its ashes and squabble with tooth and claw for burnt spoils, if they were allowed.

She would not let them. Her best way of defeating them was by helping Shar, but how could that be done?

She sat in the cave, and thought while she rested. The cave was older than the forest, and once creatures of power had dwelled here. They were gone now, they and many others of their kind, fled into even darker places of the world or else destroyed by the advance of humanity. Humanity and magic did not mix, saving some few people in whom it ran from days of old, and the blood in them called out for it, and the magic of the land woke at their thought.

Of the gods, she recked little. Their power was great, but like other creatures of the Old World they kept to themselves and let humanity fend for itself. So it should be, for a people who could not fend for themselves were a people asking to be enslaved. The world was better without gods, yet they had their uses and those with the secret lore could still converse with them and learn what was hidden to mortal sight. Or borrow of their power.

Shulu breathed deeply, and rested. Her chest rattled with the incoming air though, and her heartbeat thrilled and skipped to a wild rhythm. Her heart was not what it was. Nothing was as it had been in her youth, and all that she loved was gone, save for Shar only.

She rested and calmed herself. Tranquility settled over her again, as if it were a favorite cloak to be donned at need. Only thus could she endure the troubles of the ages, and the troubles that beset her now.

At least she was safe. She did not think she could be tracked to this place, or followed. It was certain that there were those out there who sought to do so though. So far, she had eluded them.

The one central question to all her needs at the moment was how to help Shar. To that, she must turn her mind.

There was nothing she could do though. But maybe she was thinking about this from the wrong angle. Of course she could not help Shar. She was far away, and could not be reached. Except by magic. At need, that was still possible. So she had planned, and she would know when it was necessary to invoke that enchantment. Yet there was another possibility.

She could help *indirectly*. Yes, that was a line of logic worth pursuing. She need not help Shar to benefit her. Hindering Shar's enemies would accomplish the same thing.

How could that be done? The light of the full moon filtered through the forest outside, and some shafts crept through the mouth of the cave into the interior and reached for her like a memory trying to come to the surface.

She had it. It was a bold thought, but it was an omen that she considered it even at that time when the doors of possibility were open. For on the full moon the shamans gathered together, spirit to spirit, and held a ghostly conclave at Three Moon Mountain.

She considered no more. The choice was made, and to think of it further was to allow doubt to creep into her mind. Doubt was a weakness that gnawed at courage, and she would not allow that. If she could help Shar, she would, and she would risk all consequences.

Her decision made, she breathed more deeply still and felt the tranquility of the night embrace her. She was one with the shadows. She was one with the moonlight. Her heart beat in time with the rhythm of the forest, and she felt the life of a thousand, thousand creatures stir around her, and the death of the countless before whose bodies enriched the deep forest soil and were born anew in the ceaseless waves of life and death.

With a flutter of her heart her spirit broke the chains of the flesh and soared free. She passed through the stone roof of the cave, up, up beyond the tops of the whispering pines and out into the starry universe.

The Forest of Dreams lay below her. She was in the northwest of the land, and as she rose higher the empire of old came into view. Night draped the landscape, yet her spirit eyes penetrated the shadows and saw what her mortal eyes could not.

Afar were the Eagle Claw Mountains, and there she set her course, speeding through the sky and watching the land beneath flit by.

She missed this. Free of the chains of the flesh she was ageless. Magic was at her grasp, and if her power had decreased as her body aged, here it was as strong as it ever was. But in the spirit world, the power of magic was ever diminished from what it was in the physical realm. And there were dangers for one as old as she was. Her heart could stop. The magic that enabled spirit walking was hard on the body.

Beneath her, a varied landscape passed. Grasslands, forests, shining rivers, lakes, mountains and swamps. All the lands of the Cheng were within her reach, and beyond.

She saw a deer, pursued by wolves with others waiting ahead to spring a trap. An owl flitted silently from one tree to another, but not as silently as she. In the grass rodents stirred, seeking grains on the ground and climbing stalks to reach seeds not yet fallen. A ghirlock bird careered across the lower skies, and a flock of ducks twirled and twisted through the air, calling as they flew and seeking new wetlands in which to feed.

A fox she saw, secretive and shy, following some trail of scent. For all its seemingly timid nature, it was bold at need, and when seen by a human it was confident in appearance, not alarmed nor scared, and went unconcerned about its business and got out of sight quickly yet without haste. Like the fox she must be if she were to survive what she planned.

The Eagle Claw Mountains rushed upon her, and she slowed. It was Three Moon Mountain she sought, and she found it swiftly.

There were wards. They existed for such as she, and they could bring death to the unwary and certainly warn the shamans of an intruder. They were nothing to her though. Was it not she who had taught their uses to the shamans long ago? They had not reached her mastery. Yet still, she must be careful. Pride was a step on the road to death.

She passed beneath some wards, and above others. She could not see them, but she could feel the magic as a person might feel the brush of cooler air against their skin. They were of different kinds, and some were traps: made obvious in one place so as to lull wariness and be snared by a well-hidden one unexpectedly nearby.

Three Moon Mountain rose before her now, dark and majestic. She knew its secrets. She knew what the people of the Cheng did not, for once she was a shaman herself.

She felt the power of the mountain, for there was great magic here. It had nothing to do with the shamans, yet they used it as they could. It was older by far, and they did not understand it properly. Nor did she. Yet she respected it more than they, and was wary of it.

It was to the summit she went. There were countless halls tunneled and burrowed through the mountain, and there was much there the Cheng people did not know. But the conclave was held upon the point of the mountain. The summit was not large, yet it was a flat area large enough to hold them all, at least in spirit form.

She did not think a person could ever climb this high and live. The cold was bitter. The way was perilous beyond measure. The air was thin and a man might gasp for breath and yet suffocate for lack of it.

Shulu came among her sworn enemies. They would discover her soon, but not straight away. She had time, for in the form of spirit she could take on any visage. So it was that she passed among them as Shaman Drasta of the Two Ravens Clan. The man was dead. This she knew by her arts and good planning, yet she did not think the other shamans knew yet. Certainly not the bulk of them. It was not a perfect disguise, but it was the best opportunity to pass undetected for a while.

The shamans formed a ring, centered around the elders who stood in the middle. Above, the cold stars glittered brightly in the thin air. There was a sense of danger here. Magic lay below them. To the sides was a precipice that would cow them all if they were here in the flesh. Most of all, this place was ancient. It was a place of the gods, and mortals trespassed here.

Shulu hung back in the outer circle of shamans where the less powerful stood. In the middle, one of the elders was speaking, but she paid him no heed. She drew upon her magic. She felt it quicken to life. All was different in spirit form, but she still had power here, and especially that of illusion.

Out of the thin air and starlight she formed an image. It was of one she knew well, and one the shamans knew too. Some of them were ancient. Some were old enough to remember this man while he lived, and if they had forgotten their fear of him they would soon remember it.

It was Chen Fei she summoned. He descended near the elders, an image of authority, dressed in his silk robes, girt with the Swords of Dawn and Dusk, crowned by a circlet of fine gold and diamonds.

The emperor's eyes blazed. Violet they were, piercing as the stars in this high place, and his voice was as thunder when he spoke.

"Ye dogs!" the emperor cried, though few there were in the conclave who might discern it was an illusion rather than his spirit. Yet all knew his likeness, even if they had not seen him in the flesh.

"I curse you from on high, cowards, assassins, corruptors of the people."

As the image of the emperor spoke, Shulu caused him to raise up his arms toward the heavens. There clouds gathered and roiled, and from their midst lightning flashed. It arced, silver white, reaching from the sky to the peak of the mountain. It struck. One of the elders flung up a shield of fire, and saved himself. But the magic scattered into the crowd and wounded many, for those who spirit walked might be injured or killed even as in the flesh.

"Your schemes are as naught! My descendant comes for you. Shar Fei will break you. She will scatter you to the winds on the ashes of your defeat. The signs are in the stars, and the spirit world whispers of the doom that will befall you. Verily, the death you long deserved now rushes upon you!"

Shulu grew weak, but she had done enough. Less was more here. The longer she kept this going the more shamans would realize it was only illusion, so she let image ascend into the clouds.

Chaos had broken out among the conclave, and the shamans fled back toward their bodies. This would delay whatever decisions they would make, and seed doubt and fear in them so as to slow down their communications in the future. That would give Shar more time.

Taking advantage of the situation, Shulu fled even as they did, pretending to be one of them. Yet even as she soared into the night she knew she was followed. At least one, perhaps more, had perceived the attack stemmed from her.

She streaked toward her body, but the cave, and safety, was far away.

10. Unrelenting

Shulu flew on the wings of night, and she sped as an arrow shot from the bow. She was stronger than the shamans. Faster. More sure of the spirit world than they.

And yet they pursued her. They were unrelenting. There were three of them, likely from the elders who ruled the shamans for theirs was the greatest power among her enemies.

And in the long years since last she had confronted them, they had gained in strength and wiles. Once, she could have outpaced them. She could not now. Nor could she return to her body without throwing them off her trail. If they knew where she reposed in the flesh, they would send their servants to kill her.

Shulu soared high into the starry sky until the world receded below. Higher than the peak of any mountain she rose, yet her foes dogged her.

She swept down, flitting among the clouds and turning back on her path, yet still they followed. They gave no quarter. They knew who she was, and a thousand years and more of hate lent power to them.

The clouds gave way, and she dropped low to dart between the tops of the trees in a forest. It made no difference. She haunted the shadowed aisles of the forest, a shadow like the other shadows, but they found her and fire darted from their spirit fingers.

Red light flared. It blinded her. Dizzy and confused, half blind, she sped away. They were after her, closer now than before.

Her vision cleared. The forest gave way, and ahead she saw a lake. Into this, she dived, driving deep into the dark waters. It was cold and alien. It was no place for a human, in the flesh or spirit. The fishes darted from her, sensing something amiss. But red light flared behind her, and the dark world was lit. She could not escape here. Not this way.

A fish sped away from her, and she merged herself with it, her spirit body one with its cold flesh. She led it into a school of others of its kind, and there she moved from one fish to another hoping to lose those who pursued her.

Her enemies were fooled, but not beaten. They separated, becoming one with fish themselves, and they hovered around the edges of the school, turning and twisting as it turned and twisted itself in the cold waters. They waited, guarding the edges, for sooner or later she must break out. The body could not endure long without the spirit to nourish it, and back in the cave she weakened. They knew it was so, and they were fresher than she, not having made the long journey she had to Three Moon Mountain.

Shulu did nothing without thought, and she never panicked. She bided her time, and when the school darted suddenly in one direction and broke up as a predator fish moved toward it, she leaped upward and speared into the sky.

The enemy were upon her, and the pursuit began again. This time she turned back toward them, throwing out fire and smoke as she flew. That surprised them, and they backed away.

Shulu was already darting high into the sky again, seeking a bank of clouds. Into this, she disappeared. If the others followed, she could not be sure. Perhaps they did and had lost her trail. Or mayhap they waited outside the clouds, ready to swoop upon her when she left.

Again, she bided her time. The clouds rolled westward, and beneath her the country changed. She floated now at the very bottom of the fogy air, and when she saw a flock of ducks pass below she took another chance.

Diving down like a falcon she became one with a duck in the center of the flock. Two of the elders pursued her. Where the third was, she did not know. But the two that were still with her were too far away to tell which bird she joined with.

She saw with the eyes of the duck. Head outstretched, she felt the beat of her wings and watched as the head swiveled first one way and then another, seeking water. It lay below in the form of a bright and winding band. It was a river, though Shulu was not sure which one.

The ducks dropped toward it and flew a long circle around it. Some landed, but others did not. Her enemies could not be sure if she still flew, yet she did and the birds came around again for another attempt.

One of the elders had gone down with the first group. Only one remained, and Shulu broke from the flock and arrowed away toward a forest in the distance.

Again, she was pursued, but she had lost two of her enemies now. The third she would lose also, but her confidence was shaken. She had not anticipated such a strong response from the shamans, and doubt began to creep upon her.

The forest was a blur of shadows and trees. She swirled through it, ever seeking the darkest paths where the tallest and thickest groves grew. In one she came across a stag, and she joined with it.

She watched through the eyes of the beast, and smelled what it smelled. Afar was the scent of wolves, but the pack had passed and gone in a different direction. It was not alarmed, yet still it scented the air for any new threat, and its gaze was constant, searching out the shadows for predators.

It shook its great head, the antlers like a crown, and mosquitoes buzzed away from its snout.

Shulu watched and waited, hidden inside a creature that was a master of concealment itself, and whose shy nature meant it was seldom seen.

She saw nothing herself. The third elder was gone. Gone or waiting. Wherever the shaman was, he had not discovered her, and the forest was too large for one set of eyes to guard it all.

Shulu felt her heart skip a beat away in the cave, and she knew she must act. She left the stag, and in spirit form floated through the night as a tendril of mist. She was near invisible even if there were spirit eyes to see her, but no attack was launched or pursuit commenced.

Bolder now, Shulu kept low to the ground and headed northwest back to the cave. As she went, she flew higher and higher until it seemed the stars were but the ceiling of a room. Looking around from this vantage she still saw no pursuit. She had lost the third elder, yet there was still a seed of doubt in her. She could delay no longer though.

She streaked across the sky toward the cave.

In a rush, she entered her body. The frailties of the flesh assaulted her, and she felt the sting of tears at what time had wrought upon her body.

Worse was the cold. Spirit walking brought the body to the brink of death, and her limbs were as ice and her teeth chattered. In her chest, her heart beat thin and thready, like a sting that could be cut at any moment. A great tiredness swept over her, and though she tried to stand she instead fell.

Sleep took her, and death was close. It was best not to sleep after spirit walking, for the world of dreams and the world of the spirit were near to each other, and it was easy to slip from one into the other and never return if the body was ill.

Yet she drifted away, and for once her power of will was not enough to sustain her.

11. Choose Now

Shar had seldom felt so tired in her life. Never had she wished to be alone so much, and to wash and clean herself up. She must look awful, and yet none of that mattered in the slightest.

She was the emperor-to-be, and these men did not care if she looked pretty. They were not interested in her aches and pains. All that mattered to them was that she was strong. Only in that could they trust, and she did not blame them. Anything less could not hope to stand against the might of the shamans, for if she fell they would fall with her.

She gave them what they wanted. When she felt tired, she made a point of appearing energetic. When she felt like crying over what had been done to her, she smiled. It was not for them. It was not for her. All that she did was for the Cheng nation.

"Is it true," she asked Nahring, "that the hill tribes torture an Ahat whenever they find them?"

"It's true," the chief of the Smoking Eyes Clan replied. "Not in my lifetime, so far as I know. There are few in the hills that would hire an assassin, and we're small clans and distant from central Cheng lands. There's little to be gained by it. But in the past we've tortured the few that were ever caught. They're hated. And always, like the other tribes all over the land, we seek to find where the Ahat originate from. They're a blight upon our nation, and if we could we would destroy them."

Shar looked at Nerchak, still tied over the horse. He had said nothing, nor moved.

"You're in for a bad time. I promised to kill you myself, but it seems the hill tribes will do it. Eventually."

She almost felt sorry for him, but then she remembered what he had done to her and hardened her heart. Fear was a weapon, and if she showed weakness here it would give strength to her enemies who would seek to kill or capture her again. Likewise, the fate of Nerchak would give them pause.

Nerchak was untied from the horse, but the bonds about his wrists remained. He said no word. He held his head high, but looked at none of them as he was taken into custody by members of each chief's retinue.

Kubodin looked at Shar appraisingly. "Time for some quick decisions. I suggest we stay here and rest a while, and allow you to refresh yourself. Then we must ride back swiftly to Two Ravens land. Other chiefs will be arriving for the ceremony to make me chief."

They all agreed to this, and Shar was grateful. Kubodin would have returned instantly, but he saw how tired she was and through her act. He was giving her the rest she desperately needed.

The men sat around and took their ease. Asana drew her aside, and led her to a spot near a tree.

"Sit," he suggested, "and I'll tend to your injuries. I'm not a healer, but I'm not without skill either."

That she knew. It was a custom among the Cheng that those who learned the highest arts of fighting also learned how to heal, especially injuries. The knowledge of how to give and how to alleviate injuries was one and the same, and to be a good warrior demanded knowledge of bones and muscles, and how to strike with hand or blade to bypass their protection and impact the vital organs. It followed that learning how to heal the aftereffects of such injuries made a person a more efficient warrior also.

He drew a cloth from beneath his cloak and dabbed it in water from a waterbag. Gently, he started to wipe away the caked blood on her face. Then he worked on her hair. This hid one of her worst wounds, and she winced several times as it was cleaned.

Despite the pain, she realized Asana was very gentle. He was a strong man. Even so, his touch was smooth and deft, and this was one of the reasons he was such a fine swordsman. Strength was good, but it was inferior to that relaxed and supple strength of a true swordsman.

"We were worried about you," he said.

She flashed him a tired grin. "I was worried about *myself*. But there seems to be something to this destiny idea. Luck favored me, and I was able to use it to overcome him. It was chance though. I might never have had it, but I got lucky."

Asana did not cease cleaning her wounds and washing her face, but he looked thoughtful.

"Destiny? Maybe. I think instead it was your own courage. Whatever chance you got, it was still you who acted on it. Fate can't do that for you."

She shrugged. "You might be right. Think on this though. Despite all the potential damage being abducted has done me, I still ended up here. With many of the chiefs of the Wahlum Hills to greet me, and to see that I rescued myself without their help and defeated an Ahat, alone and while a prisoner. No plan, nor words nor actions that I could have thought up myself could have convinced them to join me more than that. If it wasn't fate, I don't know what it was."

He did not answer that. There was no way he could. Destiny and luck always ran the same race, side by side, and it was impossible to tell one from the other.

"It looks like your nose was broken," he said. "Can you breathe properly?"

"It was. I straightened it when I got free."

She could barely even recall doing that. So much had happened, and it seemed like a small thing compared to the rest. She saw his eyes widen a touch though, which was more surprise than he usually showed.

"We can stay here and rest for as long as you need," he offered. "The chiefs won't begrudge you that."

She shook her head. "No. Maybe they won't, but I will. Time is slipping through my fingers, and the enemy won't be acting at leisure. I can delay no longer in raising a bigger army, and marching."

"You seek to bring war to the shamans already?"

"No. Not if I can help it. I just want to be somewhere they don't expect me, and if I can inflict damage on them and grow my reputation while I try to gather more and more tribes, all the better. I can't do any of that in the Wahlum Hills."

When Asana had finished he sat quietly beside her. She did not speak either, but merely took the opportunity for a short rest. No one would notice this, and they would think he was talking to her. She knew that this was his way of giving her whatever rest she was willing to take though, and she appreciated it. Whatever else may befall her, she had found true friends in Asana and Kubodin.

The sunlight was warm on her face, and she felt strength returning to her. It was also marvelous to be free of dried blood and grime, or at least as free as she could be until they reached a creek where she could bathe.

She stood up. "Thank you, Asana. When Shulu chose you and Kubodin as my companions, she chose well."

Asana did not answer, but merely acknowledged her words with an inclination of his head.

She strode over to the others. "Time to be going," she said. "There's much to do, and Kubodin won't go through his chief's ceremony sitting around here waiting for me all day."

They mounted and began the trek back to Two Ravens country. She saw that Nerchak was on foot now, though his hands were still tied, and that fresh blood was on his face. She gazed at him coldly, and then looked away. He had taken his chances when he abducted her, and the gamble had not paid off. The consequences were on his own shoulders.

The ponies traveled quickly, and at times the retinue of foot soldiers fell behind. Shar was keen to get ahead, and would have taken the risk, but Kubodin slowed her down.

"We're not in Two Ravens land just here. Best for us all to stay together."

Reluctantly, she agreed. Her gaze fell on a man who rode with the chiefs, but his clothes were simpler and the air about him different.

"I know you," she said to him. "You're the hunter I met a while back when I came into the hills with Kubodin."

He grinned widely, pleased that she had not forgotten him.

"This is Radatan," Kubodin told her. "No one could find your trail except him, and that we're here at all is thanks to him alone."

Shar thought for a moment, then she drew her pony to a halt and dismounted. She walked over to the hunter, and acting on instinct alone did something she had not anticipated. She bowed deeply to him, and then spoke with deep formality.

"Radatan of the Two Ravens Tribe. You have done me a great service. But I ask more. There are those who would kill me, and I have need of a trusted guard even as my forefather did. It is not the reward you deserve, but will you be the first member of that guard? Will you place your life in jeopardy to protect me? It will be dangerous, and it is a burden. Will you accept?"

The hunter seemed stunned. In turn, he dismounted and bowed to her.

"Emperor-to-be. I accept. You could not know this, but the story in my family is that one of our ancestors was a bodyguard to Emperor Chen Fei. I humbly accept, and no greater reward could be offered to me."

Shar was as surprised as Radatan had been. Her thoughts returned to the idea of fate as they mounted and rode ahead. Surely, this was an example of it. The moment the hunter had told her of his ancestor, it was like a bell ringing in her head. It was as though the world had come into perfect alignment, and the past and the future had become one for an instant. It was as though a step in some great plan that she could not see had come to fruition.

In truth, Kubodin and Asana were already her protectors. They had sworn as much to Shulu, but Kubodin was a chief now with other responsibilities, and Asana was … he was Asana Gan, and no one asked him to be their guard. It was not fitting.

They climbed deeper into the hills, and a fog rose up about them, thick and clammy. It seemed to her that it was always like this here, but she liked it. The fog muted sound, and hid the landscape around them. It hid her too, and should there be enemies about it would be impossible for them to find her.

She did not think there could be enemies here yet. Not sent by the shamans anyway. That did not mean though that there were not some here already. She had won the chiefs over, at least into recognizing her as emperor-to-be. And she knew she had great support among the people. Even so, there would be those here who wished her harm, and she could no longer ignore that. She had once, and it had nearly cost her everything.

The chiefs had recognized her. That was not enough though. What counted was what they were willing to do for her. It was an issue that needed to be discussed, and she decided to bring it to a head now.

"Chiefs," she began, "you've recognized me as emperor-to-be. As heir of Chen Fei, that is my right. You have pledged yourselves to obey me. All of which is fine, but in reality is nothing more than noises on the wind without the actions to back it up."

Dakashul laughed. "Straight to the point!" he said. "I like that, but Kubodin didn't tell us you were like that."

"Better to find out for yourselves," Kubodin muttered with a grin.

Shar shrugged. "Actions speak louder than words, gentlemen. And if we're to free our people from the claws of the shamans, strong actions will be needed. I need to know now who I can truly count on. Later will be like trying to saddle the horse after it's run to the opposite corner of the field."

Nahring, solemn as always, pursed his lips as he thought.

"What do you wish? To gather our armies and march?"

He might be solemn and softly spoken, but his mind was sharp.

"The shamans won't be waiting," Shar answered. "They fear me. They have since before I was born, but now they see who I am and what I'm capable of. They *must* destroy me. They *must* destroy any who join with me so as to deter all others. So there'll be an army marching toward us as we speak. If you truly believe in our cause, you'll gather your armies and prepare to march. We have to leave the hills, and soon."

"We'll need time to consider that," Sagadar said.

He would have gone on to say more, but Shar shook her head.

"You have no time. Choose now, for the fate of your tribes depends on swift action. If you don't prepare to march straight away, your tribes will be destroyed. If you won't commit in deed as well as word, I'll leave and gather an army elsewhere. It may seem that I'm being harsh, but it cannot be any other way."

They looked at her thoughtfully, and she held each of their gazes in turn with her violet eyes.

12. Queen of the Gods

Surprisingly, it was Dakashul who answered Shar's question.

"I can gather my warriors swiftly, emperor-to-be. I understand your need. In war, the enemy who is slow to act is the enemy who loses. And I'll march wherever you lead."

Kubodin offered the same thing next, and she realized he had deliberately hesitated in order to put at least one of the other chiefs under pressure of answering first. That way it could be seen that it was not always him that offered her support. They all answered in the end though, even Sagadar, and they all agreed to do as she wished.

When they reached Two Ravens land and Kubodin's village, there were other chiefs there who had been invited to the chiefdom ceremony. Shar wasted no time, but spoke to them passionately about the need to overthrow the shamans, and whether it was because of her violet eyes, or that she had already gained the support of some of the most respected chiefs, they bowed to her as well and pledged their loyalty. And their warriors.

Shar had an army now, and not a small one. It was as nothing compared to what the shamans might throw at her, but it was a start. Word had been given to gather, and men would soon be marching over every ridge and in every valley of the Wahlum Hills to assemble on the western foothills where she had just come from.

The shamans of those tribes would interfere, if they could. But word of her coming had spread through the hills as a fire, and it seemed the populace was behind her. The shamans could not fight against that.

The night of the ceremony came, and all that day a great column of Two Ravens warriors, headed by Kubodin and the other chiefs, wound their way up to the ridge where the two sacred hills of the tribe rose high into the air.

It was a strange feeling for Shar to be part of this. It was not like the swearing in ceremony of the Fen Wolves that she knew, but it was said that all over the land the clans followed age-old traditions for this, some of them dating back to the time of the Shadowed Wars.

They climbed the winding and rugged path that led to the top of the right-hand hill, looking down into the sacred valley of the tribe. Dusk was falling, and a bonfire sprung to life on the tops of both hills at the same moment.

The procession of warriors, women and children all seemed subdued. Even Kubodin was, and he had an air about him of regalness. She had seldom seen it, but she knew it was always there beneath his mischievous personality.

The night was deep in the heavens by the time they reached the crest of the hill. The bonfires that had been lit had burned down to sullen embers that cast a ruddy glow. Each hill looked like a head, with a red eye that gazed down into the valley below.

The ledge that ran out and looked like a raven's beak was ill lit, and dangerous. It was there she knew Kubodin must go, and she feared for him. Any misstep was death, and the fall was great to the rocks below. It was a thing that she had heard whispered on the way up here, that a chief who was not approved by the gods would fall.

It was superstition. Or was it? Shulu had said little about these ceremonies. She had always said though that where there was a legend, a seed of truth was behind it. So it might be here. Yet if so, none could be a better chief than Kubodin. He would be safe. Even so, she feared for him.

The elders of the Two Ravens Tribe gathered around Kubodin, and they chanted eerily into the night. Shar could not understand the words. It seemed to her that it was not the Cheng tongue, or if it were it was strange and distorted. Or, it may be, it was the tongue of her ancestors as they had spoken it in ages past, remembered for such an ancient rite as this, and it was the language she herself spoke that had become distorted over the long years.

Drums began to beat from the shadows behind them, and the noise of more drums rose up from the crest of the other hill. A slow throb filled the air, and the embers flared to life as something was thrown upon them. Whatever it was, it burned brightly, and the light of it was green, then red then a flashing white that was nearly blinding.

The fires burned low and sullen again, but there was a scent in the air now of burned herbs. Shar did not breathe deeply. Shulu had said that hallucinogenic plants were used in some ceremonies. That was what she smelled, and the lights were caused by the burning of strange minerals mined of the earth and ground to powders.

The chanting of the elders grew to a crescendo. It lifted up into the dark skies, and even as it did so it suddenly ceased and the beating of the drums with it.

Kubodin walked toward the ledge, and before him was a kind of walkway formed by the chiefs of the other tribes. He drew his axe, and he kissed the blade before he laid it down on the grass.

"Let no man touch it," he said, then he removed his tunic and walked through the column. The skin of his back was crisscrossed with scars, and even in the dim light Shar could see them. Small wonder he hated the nazram, for it must have been they who did this to him before Asana saved him.

To Shar's surprise, the chiefs drew their swords and struck at him. She began to leap forward, but Asana gripped her arm.

"Watch!" the swordmaster commanded.

The blows were pulled. They did not bite into Kubodin's flesh, though he would be bruised by it, and in places where the edges of blades had caught his exposed skin the blood ran freely.

Kubodin ignored it, and walked as though in a trance until he had passed through.

"I've seen this in other tribes," Asana whispered. "It represents an ancient time when the chieftainship was claimed by battle."

Shar felt sudden pride for her friend. He had endured much to reach this point, and now he walked proudly out onto the ledge. No one followed him.

It seemed to Shar that Kubodin went right to the very tip of the stone beak. One more step, and he would plummet to his death. Yet he sat down cross-legged, chanted a phrase in that tongue she could not understand, and then went quiet.

Even at that moment there was a loud hiss as water was cast over the burning embers. Again and again this happened, and the embers darkened and the world was plunged into deep shadows again.

Everyone withdrew, but Kubodin must sit where he was in the dark and contemplate the future of his tribe and how best he could serve it. Thus he must stay, in peril of his life should he fall asleep or move from his position, until the light of dawn came.

Most of them withdrew some distance away, but Shar and Asana as Kubodin's friends, and the chiefs and the elders of the Two Ravens Clan stayed closer, but they spoke seldom and only in whispers. Nothing could disturb the ritual.

Shar waited with patience. And even as Kubodin must think of the future of his tribe, so she considered the future of the Cheng nation.

As time passed the stars thinned and were then blotted out by a cover of clouds. It rained. At first, it was a drizzle, but then it grew heavier. A wind came with it, whipping rain into Shar's face.

It was uncomfortable for her, but rain and wind could kill Kubodin where he sat. One mistake was all it would take. One error of judgement and he could slip and fall.

She heard nothing though, save the noises of the night. Surely he would yell if he slipped? Perhaps not. When death came for Kubodin, he would greet it in silence, or maybe even try for a joke. That was his nature, and she loved him for it.

The rain passed. The wind died down. At length the bank of clouds rolled away and the stars came out again. The valley below was obscured by more than the night. A thick fog lay there like water in a basin, yet up here where a hint of a breeze remained, it was clear.

"The dawn comes," whispered Asana.

Shar could not see any sign of it. It still seemed full night to her, and yet within a little while she noticed that indeed the eastern sky began to gray.

She looked out to the ledge, but could see nothing. It was obscured, and whether Kubodin still lived, she could not tell. It was no doubt a harrowing experience, and what had caused the ancients to choose such a ceremony as this was beyond her. She did remember Shulu saying something though. *Nothing that is easily attained is respected.* Perhaps that was the answer.

Her eyes adjusted to the growing light, and with relief she saw at last the vague outline of Kubodin. He sat exactly as he had earlier.

The dawn quickened. She could see him better, his head bowed a little with tiredness. But then he looked up, almost startled.

There was nothing to see, and yet the little man sprang to his feet as though he were on safe ground and his hand dropped to where the haft of his axe would normally be, but found nothing.

Shar stood. All around her others did the same, and there was a murmur of surprise. A rooster crowed somewhere far away, and a chorus of birds sounded from down below in the valley.

Then there was a light. It was not the sun, nor as bright. It was golden in hue, and it sprang to life in the very air some twenty paces ahead of Kubodin. What it was, Shar could not guess, but Asana whispered nearby.

"A god joins into the ceremony."

Shar studied the figure. Shulu had told her of the gods, and she knew them by their likenesses and character. That did not mean much though, for the gods rarely appeared, even less in the last thousand years, and they were unpredictable.

The figure swelled in size, now towering above Kubodin, but the little man held his ground apparently unconcerned. He merely pulled his trousers a little higher with the rope belt that held them up, and waited.

Some of the light faded, and Shar could see the figure more clearly. It was a woman, clad in white with a golden belt of linked chains and a circlet of beaten gold on her brow. Her hair flowed back into the air behind her, gold also, but tinged with a ruddiness like the embers of a fire. Most startling of all were the double horns on her head, curving back like a ram's.

Shar knew who it was, and the whispering of her name was on many tongues. It was Uhrum, and she was not any god but the queen of the gods.

"Hail, Kubodin, Chief of the Two Ravens Tribe," her voice boomed, and though it was soft and feminine yet still it carried far and Shar would not be surprised if it were heard even down in the valley below.

Kubodin went down upon one knee, touched the stone with the tips of his fingers in a strange gesture peculiar to his tribe, and then straightened.

"I greet you, Queen of the Gods," he intoned. "And I am humbled that you grace my rite of passage to the chieftainship."

"You are now a chief, and will be more beside. The gods are pleased with you, and you bring honor to your people. Know this though, mortals." As she spoke she looked around at those gathered, and most fell to the ground in worship. Shar felt the urge, but instead she only knelt as Kubodin had done, and she noted Asana did likewise.

The gaze of the goddess lingered on her, and Shar felt the weight of a mind heavy as a mountain scrutinize her, then it was suddenly lifted and she found she had been holding her breath.

"Know, O mortals, that chance and fate charge the air. All things are possible now, and fate that can take many paths will run in due course into the one, immutable, unchangeable, unfaltering road that you know as *Time*. This can bring glory or woe. Or both. The shamans are as the night, and the emperor-that-might-be is the day. They cannot endure each other, and the one must fall and the other prosper. So the stars sing, and thus the grinding of the stones deep in the earth mutter."

Queen Uhrum raised both her arms and reached high into the air.

"Behold!" Even as she spoke it seemed that a curtain of shadow came down over the heavens and the pale sky was dimmed once more. Yet against that dark backdrop vast images formed.

Shaw saw scenes of mighty battles, and saw herself wielding the Swords of Dawn and Dusk. Against her came the shamans and their armies, and behind them rose Three Moon Mountain. Shar was a storm assaulting their fortress, but they cast down spears of lightning upon her. Whether this was a vision of the future, or symbolic of the battle being fought, she did not know. Even so, a chill ran through her.

On both sides were mighty armies, and it seemed all humanity was massed there, fighting for one side or the other.

"Mortals!" Queen Uhrum declaimed. "Great battles lie ahead, and days of dark, deceit and sudden joy. Know, however, that the choices and powers must all be yours, and yours alone. The gods have held council and agreed not to interfere lest the world be rent asunder and hurled, shattered and lifeless, into the void."

The goddess lowered her hands and the vision of the great battles faded as the light of the new day filled the sky again.

"Your fate is your own to choose, yet be wary. The gods have agreed not to interfere, but there are those whom the shamans will call upon with dark rites, and they may render aid beyond the casting of spells. Beware! But know that no dark magic is brighter than the courage of your souls."

The goddess began to recede then, growing smaller and fading away until there was a last glimmer of golden light and she was gone.

A few moments Kubodin lingered on the ledge, then he turned, carefully, and walked over to them. He retrieved his axe, picking it up carefully as though he had greatly missed it.

"Well then, that's done," he said. "Now we march to war."

13. The Serpents Strike

Shulu slept, and in her dreams she knew she was on the brink of death.

The void was before her, impenetrable and unfathomable. It called to her like a person who had climbed a great height and looked down. She had the sensation that she was already falling, or inevitably would.

She tossed and turned. Drawn to death on the one hand by the feebleness of her body, yet called to life on the other by the power of her will that had never yet let her down.

Life won, and she slowly came to wakefulness. She had not rested properly, nor regained her strength. Yet she had gained some, and the exhaustion of her flight from Three Moon Mountain and the pursuit that had followed was lessened.

It was still there though. She sat up in the cave, and her body ached. She still felt cold too, for the touch of death put ice in a person's blood, and it was slow to thaw.

Doubt nagged at her. She had returned to her body and had not been followed. But could she be sure of that? The last elder who had hunted her had been canny. She *thought* she had thrown them off the trail, but she could not be sure.

Shulu tried to stand, but dizziness assaulted her. She should move from this place lest she was followed. If so, then the elder could alert their servants who were near to attack.

How long had she slept? She was not sure. Hours she felt, but it might easily have been a day. It was night outside, but was it the same night or the next one?

She felt the ashes of the fire she had set in a ring of stones in the cave. They were cold. She had gathered a store of fuel though, and she placed some in the ring and risked a tiny spark of magic to set it alight. Even that felt sluggish to her, and she knew her powers were not yet returned to normal.

The fire caught though, and soon it was that ancient magic that humanity had discovered long ago. It was warmth and light and comfort. It lifted the spirit and eased some of her aches and pains. It reminded her of life and all that she had always fought for.

Even so, she felt the shadow of death still cling to her, and the memory of all those whom she had lost was near to her thoughts. She would join them. Soon. But not yet, if she could help it.

The fire warmed her, and it cheered her also. In her youth, she would already have fled this cave and gone elsewhere, but she just accepted her current limitations. That was the wisdom of age. Nevertheless, she grew uneasy.

Something was wrong. Some instinct warned her, and her heart fluttered in her chest. She drew a deep breath, and stood. Even as she did so, she saw movement at the mouth of the cave.

With certainty, she knew that last elder had not been fooled, and now they had summoned servants close by to kill her. It would be no harder in the Forest of Dreams than elsewhere. The shamans had servants across the land.

There were at least a dozen, and they filed into the entrance slowly, swords drawn. They were nazram. That she could tell instantly. A moment later, she knew more. Some of them were Ahat. She did not need to see the serpents tattooed on their arms to know that. It was evident in the way they moved, the look of death in their eyes, and the fearful glances the nazram gave them.

She was blocked off from escape, but she kept calm and let the fire burn. It would be her friend soon, for yet one more of the many reasons she loved it.

"Have you come to kill an old lady?" she said, making her voice tremble as though in fear. Duplicity was her friend also.

One of them answered, and Shulu marked him for death. She had heard his voice once before, long years ago by the measure of his kind, and he had nearly killed her then.

"We come to end you, witch. You'll not escape this time. And we'll make your passing slow."

"No doubt. You at least are an Ahat. But if you are alone, I can defeat you as once before. The nazram are as nothing."

Her adversary cocked his head as though in thought, and then he gave a gesture.

All around him those who were Ahat raised a hand high and let fall their sleeves to reveal the serpent tattoo on their arms.

Shulu smiled, and she stepped back slowly a few paces from the fire.

"Ah, I see that death is truly in this cave. It lives. It breathes. It is upon us in the flesh!"

Even as she spoke she unleashed her magic. The serpents came to life, and they detached from the men and darted into the air. The black bodies twined and twirled, their red tongues licked out, and then they speared toward the Ahat.

It was illusion, but neither the assassins nor the nazram knew that. They would realize it in a moment, but in the meantime they recoiled, swords swinging. More than one of them yelled out as they were struck by someone else's blade.

The momentary chaos was all that Shulu would need, if luck favored her.

Muttering words of power, she flung her arms forward and a net of magic caught the fire and hurled it at the Ahat she had spoken to. He dived toward her, seeking to avoid the attack and strike her dead in the same move, but he was not fast enough. The fire smashed into him, and wrapped around him like ropes. He burned, and as he burned he screamed.

Still he came for her, but she held up the palm of one hand and mystic power sent him reeling back among his force, and they scattered from him in horror.

Shulu was already moving. Again she uttered words of power, and smoke billowed up from the ashes of the fire. It spun and twisted, fogging the air in confusion.

All was chaos. Others of the Ahat came for Shulu, but she was not there anymore. Under cover of the smoke she fell to the ground and crawled forward. She rose in the midst of the enemy, but again she used illusion. She was an Ahat, sword in hand.

"There!" she yelled. It was not her voice, but a man's voice, and she pointed with her sword to the cave entrance. Creeping through the smoke and half-light was a vision of herself.

The men raced after her, and then she was outside. Shulu ran with them. Yet the Ahat she had set afire came for her. He had perceived her deception, and even in his agony was driven to kill her.

His sword swept down. The blade caught her on her shoulder and she staggered, but then she leaped ahead and left him behind to die.

All was chaos. Men ran hither and thither, chasing an illusion that no longer existed. Then her strength failed her, and she fell to her knees. She felt blood drip down her chest, but she drove herself up and walked into the woods, illusionary sword drawn as though she chased someone.

Dawn was in the air, and light was coming with it. Her power was fading, and she could not hold the illusion for long. She must be out of sight before the sun came up, or the tatters of her deception would fall away and she would be revealed. Nor did she have the strength left to defend herself.

Staggering again, she moved deeper into the forest. All around her she heard men crashing about. Some shouted, some hacked at bushes with their swords, trying to clear a way or thinking to route their quarry from a place she may be hiding.

There were footsteps behind her. She did not turn to look but hacked at a stand of ferns. Then an Ahat was beside her.

"There's nothing there!" he hissed. "Remember your training! Stay calm." Then he was gone, not running but striding down a shadowy aisle of trees.

Shulu staggered away in a different direction, and even as the sun began to rise the noise of the search receded. Soon, she was alone, and there was nothing to hear but the birds greeting a new day, and the wind, lonely and morose, in the tops of the trees.

Death had nearly claimed her now, not once but twice in close proximity. She cursed her age as well as the deterioration of her powers. Time was when such a company of warriors, even if they were all Ahat, would have perished and she would have sat down by the fire unfearing of any others that might come.

It was not all age. She thought of the magic she had cast upon the talisman when this had all begun. That had drained her, and always would until she lifted the spell.

That, she would not do. The talisman was all the help she could offer Shar over the miles that separated them. No, she would not lift that spell. It had not played its full part yet. All the more so because Shar had not realized what it might do. And that meant her enemies did not, either, and it might catch them by surprise when they thought victory was theirs.

Her concern for Shar grew though. If she herself, greatest of the shamans, faced death from their enemies, how could Shar hope to survive?

14. The Swift March

It was noon on the day after Kubodin's ceremony of ascending to chieftainship. Shar still thought on the appearance of the goddess, and she knew that whatever else, it had strengthened his position both within his own tribe and without. The appearance of a god was not something that had happened in living memory. It marked him as special, and though he was the newest chief of the hill tribes, he had become the most respected.

That was not what they were discussing though. They sat in a circle in his hut, and a fire burned low in the central hearth. The smoke from it was strong in the room, but most escaped through the aperture in the center of the roof.

Shar sat to one side of him, and Asana to the other. There had been much talk, but little in the way of action, and Shar grew tired of it. She leaned forward, and fixed several of them with her violet eyes.

"While you sit and talk, your enemy marches upon you. Do not doubt it. They come, and if you are not ready they will find you in these hills, and they will drench them in blood. Your villages will be razed, and your people scattered into the deep valleys and hunted."

"What would you have us do?" one of the new chiefs asked.

"Only what must be done. Send word to your armies to hasten. They already gather, but they will be too late. They *must* hurry."

Kubodin nodded. "Do it. The Two Ravens Clan will be waiting for you on the foothills in the arranged spot."

Whatever resistance there was in the hills to Shar had seemed to melt away at the appearance of the goddess. She thought that was an irony, for Uhrum had proclaimed the gods would take no part in events. Yet her appearance had done as much as violet eyes and swords of prophecy to assure them she was the heir to Chen Fei and that this was their moment, and maybe the only moment they would ever have, to throw off servitude to the shamans.

And yet why had the goddess appeared at all? Why was there a need to proclaim the gods would not help either side? Surely that indicated that the will of the gods was not unanimous in this. Some must have favored helping one side or the other. It gave Shar an uneasy sense that more was going on than was said, and that the shamans had tried to use their influence to invoke the aid of certain gods who favored them.

At any rate, Kubodin had informed the chiefs where they must bring their armies. Messengers had already been sent with the seals of the various chiefs to set the march in motion. Now, orders were given to make it happen fast.

The chiefs discussed various other things, paramount among them the worry that while they led their armies away someone would take the opportunity to raid or conquer another tribe. It was this mistrust that the shamans always cultivated, for the tribes coming together and cooperating was one of their greatest fears. Even so, it seemed that the hill tribes were less prone to this than others, and they gave solemn oaths to each other that they would take no such action, and those left to rule in their absence would take the same oath.

When they were nearly done, Shar broached another subject.

"The shaman of the Two Ravens Clan is dead. You must expel your own, and if they refuse to leave kill them. I will not have them travel with the army as spies, nor let them remain behind in your lands. They will fill ears with poisoned words, and plot to overthrow not just me but you who have joined me."

The chiefs agreed to this, and some seemed to Shar to greatly enjoy the idea. Others seemed to want it, but feared the power of the shamans lest they raise magic against them.

Shar did not think there would be problems. The use of magic against warriors was forbidden, although that was no guarantee. Mostly though, they would know that doing so would only turn the hearts of the tribe against them even more. And if worst came to worst, few shamans could survive an attack by multiple warriors. Steel was stronger than sorcery. That might not be the case in larger tribes with the greater shamans, but that was a problem for another day.

So began the long march to war, and Shar felt confidence rise within her. She had raised an army, and tribe by tribe they would join her as she journeyed to the foothills. There they would mass, and from there she would launch her first strike.

There was much to consider, and she did so as she marched soon after. The ponies were now given back to scouts and messengers who had greater need of them. She and the chiefs walked, for the warriors must walk and they better respected commanders who endured what they themselves endured.

There was much planning to be done. An army needed equipment and food. Shar would rely on supplies from the Wahlum Hills, at least at first. But she knew she must give warriors motivation to fight, and throwing off the shamans was not the only one. Plunder and booty were good motivators as well, and there would be tribes that would refuse to accept her. It was not what she wanted to do, but no one became emperor without it. And if she did not become emperor, then the shamans would continue to enslave the land. It seemed that sometimes there were no good choices, only ones that served a greater good in the end. Even so, the shamans would bear the brunt of this. It was said they accumulated gold like a bee gathered pollen, and she would target them and let the army seize their wealth.

That was not all. By targeting shamans, preferably by killing them, she would spread fear among the enemy. That might force them into rash decisions, and this was a game where one mistake could be the last ever made.

They reached the foothills and established a camp. Straight away Shar sent messengers to the Green Hornet Clan explaining what was happening and requesting they gather their army and help.

What the Green Hornets would do though, no one could be sure. There was little contact between them and the hill tribes, and what contact there was seemed for the most part to be hostile. She did not have high hopes, and it did not help that they had not met her.

As they traveled, and now as they waited for the rest of the army, Radatan was always at her side. She trusted him, for she knew Kubodin liked him, and Kubodin was an uncannily good judge of character. Radatan might not be the finest warrior in the hills, but he would be good, and he would not let her down. That she knew, but she needed more in the way of guards.

Many of the warriors looked at Radatan with a degree of jealousy. In the days of the first emperor, guarding him was seen as the greatest honor a warrior could aspire to. There were cycles of stories about the heroes who had done so, and try as the shamans had to obliterate those stories, they were favorites of the people and they endured, even if they were not told within hearing of the shamans.

That jealousy would grow, and it could be used against her. For surely she would have enemies here. Not everyone liked her, and there would be those who would serve the shamans in secret. They would say she gave the Two Ravens Clan preference.

She did not wish to give anyone preference, for as emperor she must rule them all with equal justice. So she decided that her guards would come from all the clans. In this way she found a female warrior among Nahring's retinue that caught her eye. The woman was young, but she watched her spar some of her comrades as they waited. She had extraordinary skill with a sword, but Shar wanted to test her temperament as well, and gauge if she was one of those who liked her or was merely here because it had been required of her by her chief.

She walked over, and the sparring ceased. Those gathered there bowed to her.

"You fight well," she congratulated the woman.

"Thank you, emperor-to-be."

Shar studied the other woman. She was nervous, as well she might be, but she still looked her in the eye. She had boldness, but it was not a challenging stare. So far, so good.

"Would you like to try your luck against me?"

The other woman seemed surprised, and her gaze fell to the swords of Dawn and Dusk.

"I would like that."

Shar drew her swords and held the blades aloft. "Let no one touch these. It's death to do so." She laid them down carefully on the grass a little way away, and then returned. One of the men the woman had been sparring stepped closer and bowed.

"I would be honored if you used my blade."

Shar accepted it carefully, hilt first, and gave a small bow in return.

"I shall not dishonor it," she said.

The man appreciated that. All warriors thought of their swords as something special, and often they were inherited from fathers or uncles. In the hills though, they held them in reverence. It was well to acknowledge that, for nothing could make an enemy faster than treating it as a mere tool.

Shar turned back to the woman. There was a hint of relief on her face. She would not have to face the legendary swords of prophecy, but otherwise there was curiosity. She wanted to see how good Shar was.

They faced off and began to circle each other. All around them was silence, but Shar noticed the chiefs had walked over to watch.

"What's your name?" Shar asked the woman.

"Huigar."

It was a strange name to Shar, but the Smoking Eyes Clan were different to other Cheng. They were taller, and their eyes less dark. There was blood in their veins from outside the empire.

Huigar suddenly leaped forward and thrust at her. The move was fast, but pulled quite distinctly at the end. She was taking no chances against wounding the emperor-to-be.

Shar stepped in though, deftly deflecting the blade and then ramming her shoulder into her opponent to send her sprawling.

Instantly Huigar rolled and came to her feet, her sword in a guard position before her body. She was surprised rather than angry, and Shar liked that.

"No need to hold back," she said. "Spar me just as you were your friends. You'll not hurt me."

The woman narrowed her eyes. "That's confident." Yet even as she spoke her sword leaped out again in a slash toward Shar's head.

Shar retreated, allowing her opponent to attack and display a range of her skills. She certainly had them. The woman moved smoothly, and just like Shar relied on skill rather than strength. She deflected any attack, and used the momentum from that to initiate her own. All the while she kept her calm, and never once did she look into Shar's eyes. Which was wise while fighting an enemy that might overawe you.

When it was clear that what she was doing was not working, she changed tactics. It was an abrupt and sudden change, and she moved from circular strikes to linear thrusts. Then she moved seamlessly between both, attacking high and low by turns. Even then she was not done, and sought to get in close so that she could kick.

All the while Huigar showed no emotion, though it was obvious that she must feel frustration. Yet maybe not. She might have attained that state of mind that warriors called Stillness in the Storm.

The swords rang out, and here and there those who watched clapped or shouted encouragement. Shar began to struggle now, for her opponent learned quickly and had begun to read her. In a real fight, Huigar would be dead by now, but in sparring, there was an opportunity to use the extra time to learn about an opponent.

Worse, some of those who watched might also be learning her strengths and weaknesses, and as she knew not all were her friends. It was time to bring this to a close.

Shar leaned back out of the way of a sweep for her head, then attacked herself. Her speed stunned her opponent, yet even so she retreated in good order.

Twice, Shar knew she could have killed her if she had not been holding back, and her opponent knew it too. She stepped away and lowered her sword to signal she was done.

"You have beaten me, emperor-to-be."

Shar looked into her eyes and saw pride there. They were words Huigar did not wish to say, but she was fair and she spoke the truth.

"My friends call me Shar, and you are welcome to do so."

The other woman seemed surprised, and then she flashed a smile.

"Will you teach me, Shar Fei?" She went on bended knee as was done when a student beseeched a *gan* to pass on the secrets of their craft.

"Yes. But I can do more, if you and your chief wish it." She turned around to where the chiefs watched from.

"Chief Nahring, will you release Huigar from your service? If she is willing, I would have her as one of my bodyguards."

The chief swapped his gaze from Shar to Huigar, and then smiled.

"If she's willing, I'll do so. Know, however, that you are taking from me *my* own best guard. And also my daughter."

That surprised Shar, but then looking at them both the resemblance was obvious. Huigar approached though, and she smiled again.

"I would be honored, emperor-to-be."

Shar felt instantly that she had made the right choice. It was hard for her to trust anyone given how all her life she had hidden the truth from people about who she was. What Nerchak had done had also scarred her mind. But she had to choose *some* people to trust. She could not do everything by herself.

"Then it is done," she said. "And in recompense, Nahring, to you I will give freely any gift in my power that you choose. I suggest though that you defer that debt for some while. In the future, my capacity to give will be greater than it is now."

It was not long before the armies of all the hill tribes were gathered, and it was no small force. Shar marveled at it, for here was an army capable of establishing a new power over the lands of the Cheng. It could be a power that brought peace and prosperity. It could bring justice and advances in civilization. It could do many things, if it were not snuffed out first by the shamans who could raise an army to dwarf it. And if she led it well and did not succumb to the lure of power as the shamans had done.

Shar felt that responsibility settle over her, and it was heavy. It was not enough to defeat the enemy. She must replace them with something better.

The chief of the Green Hornets arrived with his retinue as well, and that he came in person was a surprise to Shar. But when he was brought to her she read his face immediately. He would not side with her.

"Greetings, Shar Fei," he said. And though he recognized who she was, he did not bow.

"Greetings, Nassring," she replied, for she had been told his name. He was a young chief, not greatly older than her, and pride flashed in his eyes. "You are aware—"

"Don't bother," he interrupted. "I know what you do, and what you want. You will not have it."

Shar masked her features, and she showed no emotion. This was bound to happen sooner or later, and she knew what she must say. And then do, if forced.

"You realize that I cannot allow an army to remain behind me. It could attack the rear of my force, our supply lines, or the home villages of my allies in the hills while the bulk of their warriors are with me. I repeat, I cannot allow that."

Nassring spat on the ground, and wiped his lips with the back of his hand.

"I cannot allow you to undo the good the shamans have worked for. I will not. The Green Hornets are your enemy."

Shar looked at him, and then his retinue. No doubt some felt as their leader did, but she read fear in some faces and in others a certain liking. She wondered if the chief spoke for all his people.

"Then I will destroy you. Fate demands it of me, and I will do it with a heavy heart, yet you may be assured of it. You and your lands will fall to me, and your tribe will be swept off the face of the earth. Now go, and prepare your people to defend themselves."

He turned on his heel and left. He would not change his mind, that one. But Shar looked thoughtfully at his retainers as they walked away with him. There were enough of them that the truth of this conversation would be reported, and with luck fear would accomplish what otherwise must be done by death.

15. Blood on Her Hands

Shar's army marched, but she did not move to a direct confrontation. She allowed time for her force to menace the Green Hornet Clan. Time was not her friend with the shamans, but here it could allow opportunity for the overthrow of Nassring by forces in his tribe more friendly to her, and thereby spare both sides bloodshed.

They passed by several small villages, but these were abandoned. Shar did not have the heart to raze them to the ground as she should have, and she knew she must harden her heart. She would have worse decisions to make in the future.

The scouts reported it was like this in many villages, but there was evidence the tribe was gathering together in a central spot farther ahead. This might be to fight, although they had no chance of victory, so it was a strange tactic.

"Would they not be better dispersing?" she asked the chiefs.

"It's strange," Nahring agreed. "If they dispersed, no matter the size of our army we could never hunt them all down. Then they could return to their villages after we had gone."

"That's what I would have done," Dakashul agreed. "But they might really mean to fight."

Shar could not believe that. It would be the death of them, and the chance of an easier victory, if it could be called such, had to be by dispersing. Even if she razed their villages, those could be rebuilt.

Kubodin looked from one of them to the other, and then shook his head.

"You think too highly of this Green Hornet chief. It's not about what's best for his tribe. He's thinking merely of his own skin. He'll have ordered the withdrawal from the villages, and the gathering together, in order to protect his own position. He's not going to fight us, but he dare not leave his people free and away from his direct control. Otherwise, a great many of them would offer to serve Shar."

Not for the first time, Shar realized how shrewd Kubodin was, and how lucky she was to have him as an adviser. What he said had the ring of truth to it, and she felt that the moment he spoke.

It did not change anything though. She must hunt Nassring down, or leave a contingent of her army behind in order to do so while she went ahead. Either way, it was the last thing she wanted. It would slow her down or divide her force, and that made her precarious situation even worse. She had told Nassring the simple truth though. She could not leave an army behind her.

They established a camp toward dusk by a small stream. The ground was flat, but visibility was good. Scouts would patrol at night, covering a wide perimeter, and sentries would be thick close to the camp itself. It did not seem that the Green Hornets wanted to fight, but she would be prepared against any night raid just in case.

The fires of the army burned low as the night wore on, and it grew cool. There was no breeze, and the hill tribes made little use of tents. They slept beneath the stars, and Shar did not mind it. She drifted to sleep studying them, until a fog obscured some of the sky and gray tendrils came up from the creek.

She slept deep, for she was tired. Yet as though from a great distance she heard Asana yell, and it seemed to her as she woke that the swordmaster clutched the statue of Shulu in one hand and his blade in the other. The roar of battle suddenly filled her ears, and she groggily reached for her swords and began to roll to her feet. She was too late.

A man stood over her poised to strike, and she saw that it was Nassring, Chief of the Green Hornets. His grin was wicked, but more wicked was the edge of the steel blade that would bring her death.

The blade fell, and Shar sent a prayer to the heavens for mercy on her soul and someone else to save the Cheng people. Yet even as she shrank from the blow, steel crashed against steel and the sword was swept away. Radatan was there, his own weapon knocking the chief's away. And Huigar began to press him from the other side.

The chief fell back, fighting now for his own life and Shar came to her feet, twin swords in her hand, and rushed into battle. There was no time to put her boots on, and she cursed herself for trusting in the safety of any army. This attack was born of magic, else it could not have reached her, and somewhere nearby must be the shaman of the Green Hornets.

All about her there was chaos. Warriors lay dead or dying, and a fog lay over everything, but it was dispersing quickly. It was by this means that the enemy had entered the camp under cover, or it might have been a remnant of magic that transported them here. Yet surely no such magic, either way, could have brought a large force.

She was right, for as quickly as the battle began it was ending. To her left she spotted Asana, and he dived and rolled to avoid a flash of viridescent flame. The Green Hornet shaman was there, fire still dripping from his fingers as he chanted a spell. He could have attacked Asana again, but he did not. Rather, he lifted high his hands in beseeching fashion.

Shar understood. He had brought the warriors here by some mighty spell, and now he sought to return with them the same way to their camp. She leaped toward him, but he was too far away to reach. Even as she watched his form began to grow misty. She had but one chance to stop him.

With a great heave she threw the Sword of Dawn that was in her right hand. It arced through the air, beautiful, glimmering in the dull light of the dying campfires, and it struck the shaman in the chest.

The shaman reeled back, his spell broken. The sword had not hit him with the point, but just the touch of it sent pain shooting through him. Shar raced ahead. The Sword of Dusk was in her left hand, and she darted to her right as the shaman flung fire at her.

The sorcery missed her. He raised his hands again, but she was upon him. Her sword ripped deep into his belly, and then angled upward toward his heart. Blood gushed from his mouth and over her arm, but the man died and his falling weight nearly ripped the sword from her grasp.

She knelt as he fell and pulled the blade free. In the same motion she gathered up her other sword and spun around.

"Take the chief alive!" she yelled.

In moments it was all over. The enemy force had all been destroyed, save Nassring. He was wounded in several places, but not mortally.

"What happened?" Shar asked Kubodin.

The little man pointed to Asana. "Ask him. He woke us, otherwise we might be dead."

She turned her gaze to the swordmaster. "What did you see?"

"It was sorcery. Something woke me. I'm not sure what, but I sounded an alarm in time to give us a chance. It was a greater magic than I thought a shaman to a small tribe commanded, but he could only bring a few with him. That was what saved us."

Shar was not so sure of that. Asana had put the little statuette back in his robes, and he had not mentioned it. She had seen what she had seen though, and even if Asana did not understand it any better than she did, it was now beyond doubt that Shulu had cast some magic on it that helped them.

Shar turned her attention to Nassring. The chief was bound by rope now, and several wounds still bled. Her guards had not been gentle with him.

She studied him, and he looked back sullenly. It would have been better if he had been killed in battle, but she had questions for him that she must ask.

"Your shaman is dead now. He used sorcery to help kill Cheng, and his fate was sealed the moment he did that. Did he tell you what his brethren have planned?"

The chief looked away and gave no answer.

"Is there an army coming here? Is that why you defied me?"

Again, he gave no answer. Shar wanted to know what he knew, but it would only be confirmation of what she expected. There *must* be an army already on the way, sent to destroy her. She could have him tortured, but that was no way to start her leadership. Once she gave in to that, how far down the path of evil would she go? Shulu had said that even being a chief was too much power for many, and it corrupted them. Her power was already far greater, and her need for information was urgent. Both would only increase, and she must train herself now to be just, otherwise temptation would destroy her in the future.

She shook her head sadly. She would not torture him, but she could not let him live, either. He had tried to kill her, and that must be punished to show others that to try to overthrow her was death. She was emperor-to-be, and attacking her was treason to the state.

"Construct a gallows and hang him," she commanded some soldiers nearby. "Get the corpse of the shaman and hang him beside the chief."

She would not descend into evil, but she still had to harden her heart and administer justice. All the more so when it would send a message, and this was news that would travel ahead of the army and into lands she must yet march through. Chiefs and shamans would fear her, and the people would know that both could be, and had been, overthrown.

The next day the young son of the previous chief sued for peace, but he would not acknowledge Shar as emperor-to-be. It was dangerous to allow him to live, for he would seek revenge. Yet she did so. However, she asked his retinue one by one if they supported her, and the third man so questioned said he would.

"You are the new chief of the Green Hornets then. Swear to me your oath of loyalty, and bring your warriors to join my force. We march to bring down the shamans, and your tribe now has my protection. All of the tribes I have gathered to my cause are equal, and an attack on one is an attack on all. Together, we are strong. Together, we are the Cheng nation!"

The son of the previous chief was let free, yet Shar warned him that if he did anything to subvert the new chief he would be executed for treason.

By the next day the army of the Green Hornets had joined her own, and they marched toward the border of their lands. There was distrust at first, for such was the way of the Cheng tribes under the shamans. It would pass though. When they fought as one against a common enemy, something that might happen soon, they would be forged like iron into one common purpose. They would become as brothers.

It saddened Shar that she must think like this. It grieved her that her innocence was passing. All the more so for she now had blood on her hands, and yet one did not become emperor without that. This great mission she was on was changing her, and she feared it would change her more in the days ahead. She could live with that though. For her people, there was nothing she would not do, nor any burden she would not carry. And it would be for the good of the Cheng nation, so long as she did it for them and not her own ambition. That way lead to tyranny, just as it had for the shamans.

16. To Wait is to Die

The army marched next day, and they left behind them the bodies of the fallen. All were buried, save the chief and his shaman. The ignominy of them being left on the gallows would serve to keep other Cheng alive. It was a gruesome but effective message, and not just for the lands ahead.

All in her own army saw it. Most would think nothing of it, recking little of chiefs and shamans alike, so long as they were alive themselves and marched on a full belly with the prospect of gold in their future. Yet the knowledge was a seed inside them that would grow in times of hardship. The high and mighty who governed the land could be brought low. It had happened before, and they could have confidence that it would again.

Shar forced herself to look at the bodies as she marched forth near the head of the army. The crows were already in the trees in the distance, and they would feast soon. One man she had killed in battle, and the other she had caused to be executed. Their blood was on her hands, and she must not hide that from herself. She could never allow her decisions to be made without true knowledge of the consequences of them. It would dissuade her from going too far. Even so, it would not stop her from doing what was required. An emperor did not rise without bloodshed.

They passed onward, and the chiefs remained silent. They were hard men, for chiefs must administer justice and punishments as part of their daily duties. Dead bodies did not upset them, but she knew what they were thinking.

It could be them hanging on the gallows next, if they betrayed her. She now had that power, and it was a power none had ever had over them before. Even the shamans would not openly execute a chief. They might assassinate one by stealth, but not have him hanged.

Shar thought in silence as they marched over the rolling grasslands. She felt trapped. Fate had seemed a wonderful thing, if dangerous, only a few months ago. Now it was a relentless grip that forced actions from her like water squeezed from a waterbag.

The only way to proceed was to go forward, and with great speed. That alone offered hope of minimizing bloodshed and the upturning of the lives of everyone in the Cheng nation. Delay only meant that greater forces on each side had a chance to come to bear, and that would maximize destruction.

She knew where she was going though, but a plan did not last long in the face of opposition. To the south lay the Eagle Claw Mountains. They were no place for an army. It would take decades to conquer those lands, and there was little point. There were tribes there, but they were scarce and barely managed to scrape a life together under harsh conditions. They could not raise an army against her, even if they were inclined to do so, nor interfere with her supply lines. Moreover, Three Moon Mountain was not that far away, and she would not challenge the sorcery that protected that place.

To the north lay the sea. There was nothing there for her, for the Cheng, though fair sailors, did not wage war on the waters nor even use ships much as a means of transporting troops.

The only way for her was to march the narrow stretch between the two, only some fifty miles wide, toward Tsarin Fen. But to get to her own tribe, she must first deal with the Soaring Eagles that lay between her and her goal.

What reaction they would have to her, she could only guess. But she must prepare for battle. They were not one of the greater tribes, but surely the shamans would have filled out their numbers by now with nazram and warriors from other tribes, and surely they were hastening forward to catch her by surprise even as she was trying to do to them.

She did not wish to think how her own tribe would respond to her. She had many friends there, or at least those she was friendly with. Yet that was as Shar, not as Shar Fei, descendant of the great emperor. It would wound her as if she were stabbed by a knife if they did not follow her willingly, but she knew many would. The real question was would they do it in defiance of their chief and shaman?

The pace she set for the army was swift, but she walked herself every step that each warrior did. What she could do, she knew they could do also, and they would not shirk the effort and be shown up by a member of the nobility who could endure more, or a woman, especially when she was both at the same time.

There was another consideration on her mind though. Food and general supplies were more important to an army than weapons. Hungry warriors rebelled, and though she had good supply lines back to the Wahlum Hills she knew that could not last.

The bulk of the army had not realized it yet, but a time might come when they were too far away from their home to rely on supplies from that source. They must learn to do two things efficiently. Firstly, to conquer new tribes close to wherever they were operating so as to get not just an influx of warriors but also access to food supplies. And they must learn to forage off enemies as they went. Whatever was available they must gather: game, livestock, grains from the field, whatever was available they must utilize. This would not only support them, but deprive their opponents.

Another strategic goal was to overcome shamans and hostile chiefs in order to provide not just loot for the army but funds so that she might be able to buy food from tribes not directly in her path. That might not be possible, for the shamans would forbid it. But gold was a temptation that might see their orders disobeyed, and the threat of her army changing course toward those lands would intensify the situation.

When afternoon began to turn toward dusk, Shar ordered the army to set camp. They were starting to fall into a good routine, and the different tribes were beginning to work well together. Centuries of mistrust were hard to eradicate, but Shar was doing everything she could to put that in the past. The scouts of each tribe now worked together and reported to Radatan, a Two Ravens man. The sentries, likewise made up of warriors from all the tribes, reported to one leader, who was an Iron Dog. So it went throughout the camp in various workgroups, from those who dug latrines to those who cared for the ponies.

The army was growing together as an efficient unit, a single unit, and this was needed if they intended to fight well. How they cooperated now would stick with them when it came to battle. So she did all she could to break down intertribal tension and promote leaders from all the tribes equally.

Shar wondered if the shamans were doing this. It would be harder for them, for their natural impulse was always to divide the tribes. They had been doing so for a thousand years, and if they failed to adapt to this new situation then it would be harder for them to win a battle. Their advantage in numbers, and probably a massive advantage at that, might easily cover problems such as lack of trust and tension though. Or it might not. The middle of a battle would be a bad time for them to find out.

All around them the campfires of the army flickered down after the evening meal. The smell of smoke was strong in the air, although on the grasslands dry timber was in short supply. Many fires burned old dung instead, and there was no shortage of that as they had seen vast herds of wild cattle grazing during the day.

For the chiefs, a single log had been gathered and set alight with kindling. It was a large bit of timber, over a foot in girth and six feet long. The initial flames had been high, but now it was burning down and they could see each other over the top of it and talk. This they did freely, and the somberness of the morning was forgotten. Not by Shar though, and she mostly just listened vaguely as they discussed various events.

The heat from the log was intense, and she moved back a little bit. Beside her, Radatan and Huigar did the same thing. They were her shadows now, and she liked it. They had already saved her life.

When the conversation turned to the march of the army though, and how fast they were going, she focused intently on what was being said.

Kubodin was the one who brought it up. "At this rate, we'll be in Soaring Eagle lands quickly. After that, the whole land opens up to us and there are many places we might go." He looked at Shar from over the shimmering heat of the log. He must guess that she intended to go to Tsarin Fen, but where after that was a big question indeed.

Sagadar took a different view though. "Why should we continue on at this rate though? We have a large army now, and it will be hard to feed. But our supply lines are strong. We might be better off finding high ground to defend, keeping our supply lines secure, and letting the enemy come to us. Let them struggle with the difficulties of feeding a large army far from home. Let them march while we stay fresh."

Some of the chiefs seemed to agree to this, though few offered firm opinions.

Shar did not agree, but she felt a heavy weight of responsibility. These chiefs were more experienced than her, and that was daunting. At the same time, none of them had received the training she had from Shulu, a shaman who had lived more than a thousand years and who had seen an empire rise and then fall. She trusted to her teachings, and her instincts, more than to their experience.

"No," she said. "To delay is to die. To delay is to allow our enemies to gather their greater force and encircle us. Then slowly if they must, or swiftly if they can, they would strangle us. Speed is our advantage, and it always has been in military campaigns and always will be."

Kubodin agreed with her, and so did Nahring. She could see it in their faces. The others seemed undecided, but it did not really matter. In the end, they had sworn their loyalty to her and they must follow where she led. That would be tested though if she were defeated in battle. Which was all the more reason to press ahead as fast as possible. The smaller the enemy force she faced, the less risk of that happening. If she were fast enough, she just might catch them unprepared.

She fell back into silence while the others began to talk of different things. That sense of responsibility weighed on her again. She was making decisions based off limited experience, and while she did not doubt her training, she would not ignore the opinions of others either. Those opinions had value, and they made her doubt herself. At the same time, some of the chiefs agreed with her, and that was comforting.

There was only one way to find the truth of the matter though, and whether waiting or marching was the better strategy. But if she chose wrong, not only herself but her entire army would pay the price.

She brooded uneasily beside the burning log. Shulu had told her leadership would be like this, and that she must find the right balance. Not just in her choices versus the wishes of chiefs, but that an empire, which she was beginning to form, always had forces in it pulling in different directions. One mistake, and all she was building might unravel. It was not a pleasant thought, but it would not leave her.

17. All Rules Can be Broken

Skaaghul used his swamp-oak staff to help him walk. He had wanted a pony, for he was old now, and while others might call him fat it was age and rheumatism that slowed him down. Nothing more. Yet it had been decided by the others that the leadership of the army must walk to show solidarity with the soldiers. It was stupidity of course. But he had been forced to go along with it.

At least they had an army. They would need it too, by all accounts, but Shar would be crushed. How she had eluded the nazram he sent after her in Tsarin Fen, he did not know.

He glanced back at his army with pride though. The Fen Wolf warriors looked resplendent, and though he had heard grumblings about marching against Shar from the soldiers, he had suppressed that swiftly. She was outlawed he told them. She was no longer of the tribe, and she brought them dishonor. When that had not silenced some, ten lashes with the whip had. The grumbling was gone now.

The Fen Wolves were his to educate, and a time of war such as this made it easier. At least the chief understood his place. Nomgar ruled, but he knew his power came from the shamans, and he knew that in this war especially the shamans had full control. He had his own reasons to hate Shar. She had openly mocked both of them that day when she had returned to the village. And if she were allowed to gather an army, or at least a bigger one, Nomgar would lose his head. She would take his place as chief of the Fen Wolves.

That would never happen though. It was not just the Fen Wolves that marched against her, but the Soaring Eagles. And nazram had been sent from many lands. The force he and the Soaring Eagle's shaman led, with the chiefs, was large, skilled and bolstered by the nazram who were the best of the best. They would defeat Shar, and grind her into the dust. If she lived after the battle, she would be handed to the shaman elders for their amusement. Better for her if she died.

Skaaghul glanced to the right flank. As much as he did not like to admit it, there was a problem there. That was where the Soaring Eagles marched. They were a part of the army, yet the two tribes distrusted each other and would not march together. All those years of enmity could not be overcome in a short period. Yet he did not doubt they would come together when they faced a joint enemy.

That too was a problem. As soon as Shar had been defeated, discord must be sowed again lest they achieve unity by themselves even without her.

Discord should not be hard to spark to life. Nomgar and the chief of the Soaring Eagles marched with him as an example of how the armies should march together, but it was just as well that they could be seen together but not heard. they had bickered since they first met. Nomgar was vain, but Lasalath was the opposite. He was a true warrior, and he disdained the other's soft ways.

Recent news had lessened the bickering though. They had been quiet all morning since word came in that Shar had subjugated the Wahlum Hills and brought those tribes under her dominion. She had a significant army now, if only made up of wild hill men, and the rumor was that she had commenced to march herself. It was folly, of course. It would only bring on her death or capture all the sooner, but he could live with that. The sooner she was dead, the sooner he could return home. Nomgar had the right of things, and the comforts of home were better than marching beneath the hot sun and putting up with the stench of sweaty men and camp latrines.

Nomgar seemed to read his thoughts. "We'll crush her," he said. "We'll bleed her dry until she begs for mercy, and then we'll revive her just so we can do it again."

Who the chief was speaking to, Skaaghul was not sure. Of late his long-time friend had turned a bit strange and lost some of his wits. There was no doubting his hatred of the enemy though, and that was all that was needed.

Lasalath must have assumed the comment was directed at him.

"You can dream up ways to torture her after her army is defeated. Let's concentrate on that first."

The chief of the Soaring Eagles was cautious, as ever. Sometimes Skaaghul wondered if it were not caution but reticence to attack the enemy. It was something to watch out for. If the tribes of the Wahlum Hills could be turned because of prophecy and a pretty smile, then others could too. How they had allowed those simple things to influence them though, he did not understand. Who was Shar? Maybe she was descended from the emperor, but she had no skill or training. She was nothing. Yet she *did* seem to be lucky.

"I still think we should march faster," Lasalath said. "We need to force combat quickly. The longer we leave it the greater her force will grow."

Skaaghul sighed, and he did not care that his disdain was audible.

"We've had that debate already. There's no rush. We're not even sure she's got control of the hill tribes yet. Besides, we'll have our own reinforcements coming soon, and the longer we take to reach her the more our own force will grow."

Lasalath bit his lips, but said nothing. Just as well. If he pushed his ideas of marching fast and striking first any more he might just find himself punished. Nomgar had long since learned to obey shamans. It seemed the Soaring Eagle chief thought he might have actual power himself.

"What if Shar outnumbers us though?" Nomgar asked.

"Not likely," Skaaghul answered. "The hill tribes are a rabble. Those who follow her will have no discipline and probably half the warriors from each tribe will refuse to march to war. They'll have stock to tend and an appreciation of all the fine things the shamans have done for them. They'll know what's best for them, and it isn't dying in a futile war."

Nomgar did not quite seem satisfied. "But what if they *do* outnumber us?"

Skaaghul thought a moment, then turned a cold gaze on the chief.

"Then I and the Soaring Eagle shaman will use magic against them. All rules can be broken to defeat a descendant of the emperor. Have no fear. One way or the other, we'll prevail. Shar is as nothing. All she has behind her is prophecy, and that is but the last words of a dying man."

He realized as soon as he had said that last sentence that it was a mistake. Lasalath looked away and hid his face. It was the shamans who had assassinated the emperor, and their role in that was hated by the people. Moreover, he had accidently confirmed that Shar really was the emperor's descendant. It was of no matter though. They would both do what they were told. If they did not, they would be killed themselves and they knew it. Many would be eager to take their place.

All this talk did make him uneasy though. He signaled Argash, one of the leng-fah leaders to approach.

"How far ahead are your people scouting?"

The man gave him a strange look. "We're not scouting at all, Skaaghul Gan. The Soaring Eagle shaman bid us stay with the army and to fight instead."

Skaaghul had forgotten that. "Quite right. Nothing can surprise us on the grasslands. Nevertheless, send a few men out. Just in case."

18. The Legend

Shar led the army forward the next day, signaling the march herself by blowing on a gold-rimmed horn. Kubodin said it was an ancient talisman of his tribe, dating back to the empire. She believed it. She had not seen its like before, and it had a sense to it of immense age. Perhaps her great ancestor had even heard the same deep note it made.

It was barely light enough to see when the march commenced, and once again some of the chiefs pressed her to slow down.

She smiled at them. "You'll thank me if we catch the enemy by surprise. It will save many lives. At least, on our side."

So it was that she hastened over the grasslands, and the army began to bond together and work as a unit. They were no longer tribes, but *Shar's army*, a term that she had heard the warriors use as she wandered among them, and that she encouraged.

The days passed, and the bonding grew as each element of the army worked together. Shar made sure of that as best she could, even marching herself with different tribes at different times, and having the chiefs do the same. It was all so unnatural to them, but bit by bit old hostilities were forgotten and new friendships forged as they marched side by side.

It was said that of old the empire had a banner that represented the emperor, and therefore all the clans combined. What it was, Shar did not think Shulu had ever told her. Yet she could see its purpose now, and she spoke to the chiefs and made arrangements for one to be made. The tribes never used them, preferring some symbol of their totem animal or a relic of the past sacred to the clan as a common symbol. But a new banner was something that all the tribes might start to rally behind. There was another purpose it might serve too, and that would be needful soon.

That evening, by the last rays of the setting sun and the ruddy light of campfires, Shar walked among the army and spoke to warriors of all the tribes. Radatan and Huigar were with her as guards, but she had little fear. Most people she met seemed to be in awe of her, but spoke freely once she encouraged them. They liked her, and she feared no attack.

Few would dare to face her in combat anyway. She had been seen in battle, and no doubt the Two Ravens warriors who had seen her fight had passed on what they had observed of her skill. She knew she had impressed them, for few possessed her ability. She did not think it was prideful to believe so. It was just a fact brought about by the exceptional training she had received all her life.

Not only that, she had been taken captive by an Ahat and somehow managed to turn the tide against him and brought *him* back a prisoner instead. All of that was building on her legend. She was Shar Fei, daughter of prophecy, descendant of the emperor, and when she gazed at warriors with her violet eyes she sensed their awe.

That legend would be useful to her. She must cultivate it, and what better way with warriors than by martial skill. It would give them confidence in her, not just as a warrior herself but as the leader of the army. The better they trusted her, and had faith in her, the swifter they would follow orders and fight for her rather than their clan.

So when she saw a small group sparring, she saw an opportunity to do so. Not only that, it would keep her own skills sharp. If she did not train everyday herself, her ability would dull and she could not afford that. Not now when the enemy must desperately want her dead, and might use magic or assassins to try to kill her as they had tried with the emperor.

"May I have a go?" she asked.

A young warrior grinned at her. He dressed like an Iron Dog, but the others were of the Smoking Eyes Tribe. He threw her the wooden practice sword, which she caught neatly by the hilt.

"Who will be my opponent?"

A tall man stepped forward first. "I will!" The others were only a moment behind him, and Shar took that as a good sign. Warriors generally did not spar those whom they disliked. There was too much chance of the contest turning more dangerous than it should. Even with wooden practice swords, serious injuries could occur.

A clear area was made by the others stepping well back, and Shar circled her opponent, studying him. He was tall, as most of the Smoking Eyes were, and he stepped lithely. She glanced into his eyes and saw that he was watching hers. That was a mistake in battle, and she knew he was not experienced. She shifted her gaze back to his chest, and straightaway noticed his right shoulder move as he began a strike.

The man lunged at her, but Shar was already moving and her sword deflected his. In the same move she crashed her shoulder into him from the side, easily sending him sprawling as his weight had all been on one foot.

The rest of them laughed good naturedly, and her opponent rolled to his feet and saluted her. "Again," he asked.

"Let's make it interesting," Shar replied, turning to the others. "Who wants to join him and attack me two against one?"

The Iron Dog who had lent her his practice blade stepped forward faster than the others. "Me!" he said.

"Good!" she threw him her sword and he caught it as deftly as she had. Another warrior lent her a blade, and then she faced her two opponents. They grinned at her.

"You won't be grinning in a moment," Huigar called out to them. "She's faster than a hawk chased by lightning!"

One of the warriors stepped forward, but Shar was already moving. Her blade flickered out, and swept at her opponent's leg. It struck, then the tip reached up to his stomach. With a real blade, he would have been disemboweled.

Not done, Shar skipped to the side and avoided a blow by her second opponent. She dropped low again, ducking a follow up slash, and then lunged forward striking the warrior with the tip of her blade just as she had with her previous adversary.

She straightened and winked at the astonished man. There was no reaction from the crowd though, and Shar looked around. They seemed stunned, but then they broke into more cheers.

Shar offered them a little bow. "It's possible to win against two opponents," she told them. "Five is impossible though, is it not? But let's try anyway. Maybe I can take down at least a few of them."

They looked at her solemnly. Such exercises were carried out occasionally for training purposes. A warrior must train to defend against multiple attacks, but they all knew that was just fighting spirit. Actual victory could never be achieved.

The warriors chose among themselves which five would fight in the match, and Shar let them be. She calmed herself, and set her thoughts toward Stillness in the Storm.

"Are you sure you want to do this, mistress?" Radatan whispered in her ear. "You can't win against five, and losing is a bad look for who you are."

Even through her emotionless calm, Shar felt a faint smile on her lips. Radatan had taken to calling her mistress after the fashion of the high nobility in the stories of ages past. She liked it.

"I'll try to win," she murmured back. "But have no fear. If I lose, they'll still respect me for trying. All the more so because it's an impossible ask."

When her five opponents came forward, Shar called for a second practice blade for herself. It would help her, and she should practice the same way she intended to fight in reality with the Swords of Dawn and Dusk.

They saluted in the manner that was customary before sparring. It was an acknowledgment that no actual harm was intended, but that it may occur and that no ill will went with it.

Straightaway her opponents moved to surround her and make most use of their numbers. Shar darted to the side, then attacked the warrior farthest to her left. This kept the others momentarily from being able to execute their plan, and in one swift strike she was past his guard and her wooden blade whispered against his neck.

The man went down as he would in a real fight, and Shar leaped and rolled to come up behind him. Her opponents turned again to try to circle her, but once more a warrior was before her and in the way of the others. Keeping an opponent in such a position that he hindered his comrades was key to surviving a fight against multiple opponents. The moment they could surround her was the moment she lost.

The warrior jumped back trying to evade her strike toward his head. In this he succeeded, but her second blade slashed across his abdomen before he even saw it coming. It was not a killing stroke, but the first blade smashed down again knocking his own from his hand and then ran across his neck.

Even as he fell, acknowledging his loss, Shar shouldered him into the way of an opponent. Then she spun away in a different direction.

Again, she faced but one opponent. Her opportunity was slight, and she rushed in on him before the others rushed in on her. The twin swords flashed. There was a whirring in the air, and then the crack of wood against wood as her opponent blocked. But he only blocked the first few strikes. After that, he was struck multiple times.

Her opponent reeled away, and Shar spun back to face her last two remaining attackers. They were upon her, swords flashing. They had managed to come in at her from two different sides, and she retreated trying to get around the one on her left. She was tiring though, and not quick enough. She fended away a blow from the warrior on her left, then her sword swept back against him in a killing blow.

She turned to face her last remaining attacker, but too late. His blade slashed across her abdomen. It was probably a killing wound, but not instantly. Even as the wooden sword ran across her belly, her own came down against the man's neck.

A moment they gazed at each other, and then they both went down upon a knee to acknowledge they had been defeated.

The warriors gathered round were silent, then they began to cheer and yell. Shar had not won against all five. She would have died, but she had taken every single one of her opponents with her into death, and the warriors appreciated that.

Shar was pleased, but not entirely. She must keep practicing and get even better. Her life depended on it. Even so, she smiled at her opponents who were getting up now and looked around at the others.

"Remember," she said. "Losing in sparring is never a true loss. It's an opportunity to practice harder and get better. And even as we get better as warriors, so will this army get better. We might be outnumbered in the future, but never by five to one."

19. Let's Speak

Argash looked at the young recruit before him. There were many such recently, all enthralled by the idea of being a scout, of being a member of the leng-fah. They had no idea of the reality of things though, and the danger they were in. They had not seen men cut down by swords, their guts spilling out to the ground and fear in their eyes. It was because of that sort of thing that there were so many new recruits. At least to his band of scouts.

He brought his mind back to the task at hand. "These are your orders," he told the young man. "First, stay alive. You can bring no news back to us if you're dead. So be careful. Be patient. Take your time and move slowly, at least when you think you're near the enemy. Do you understand?"

"Yes, sir!"

Argash looked at him. He did not understand at all, but if he lived through his first dangerous encounter he would.

"The leadership believes," he continued, "that the army of the hill tribes is still in the hills, or close to them. I think that view is wrong. I know who leads them, and I think they're much, much closer than anyone else here says. So keep your eyes sharp."

The young man nodded. "Is it true that she was one of us, and you knew her?"

Argash was instantly wary. It was an innocent question, but it could also be a trap set by the chief or the shaman. He loved Shar like a younger sister, but he must be careful to obey his own orders and not show any sign of liking her, even less any admiration for what she had achieved.

"She was a leng-fah. She's not anymore. Assume she knows *exactly* what our scouts will be doing, where they'll try to hide and how to kill them. Do more than assume it. *Expect* it. That might keep you alive."

The scout nodded, but asked no more. It might not have been a trap after all, or perhaps he was just well coached so as not to make it obvious.

Argash continued. "At all times, be careful of traps set by the enemy. A clash of blades or the scent of smoke in the air might be designed to lure you to investigate. When you do so, you might find nothing there but enemy scouts ready to kill."

The young man did not look alarmed. He should be, for Shar was expert at these kinds of things, and would no doubt have given orders to her own scouts to hide the whereabouts of her army as best as possible.

"These are your goals," Argash told him. "First, try to find the army and establish how far away it is. That's critical information. Next, study them. How many are they? Do they seem well organized? Is their morale good? Are their sentries alert and numerous? Observe everything, and try to remember everything before you return to us."

"I will, sir."

"That's all then. Off you go."

The young man saluted and began to walk away, but Argash halted him.

"One last time," he said. "Above everything else, be careful."

"I will sir, no need to worry."

The young man left in a hurry, and Argash sighed. He did worry. He worried very much. He was likely sending the man to death, for he did not have the required skill. That was why he was not the only one being sent. In a moment, the next scout would arrive and he would have the same conversation. And then again and again.

He had called Shar the enemy, and it weighed on him. She was the enemy to the chief and the shaman, but she was not to him. Even so, who she was had come as a shock to him. Had she known all along and kept it from him?

She must have. That had been a lie, but to speak of it was to die so he did not blame her. He was not a great liker of the old emperor either, believing that no one person should ever have so much power and that if they did it would corrupt them from within. Yet that belief was founded on what he had seen of chiefs and shamans, so he was no great liker of them either.

His great grandfather was chief of the Fen Wolves, and the family stories that had come down to him were a warning of the danger. None of it mattered though. He was a leader of the leng-fah, and he had been given a job to do. Anything else would see him killed.

But he could not help thinking about Shar. Regardless of her birthright, he had discovered that the shaman had tried to have her assassinated in Tsarin Fen. He did not even know who she was at the time, and that was unforgivable. It was only after rumors that someone had at last found the twin swords of the emperor that it was revealed to be her, and that it was admitted who she claimed to be. They would not say that she actually *was* the descendent of the emperor, but looking back at all that he knew of her, and the iron of which she was made, he could believe it. She was courage and determination all rolled up into a ball of fire, and she would burn them like the sun if given half a chance.

She could not beat them though. The shamans were too strong, and the hordes of the Cheng would be mustered against her and whipped into a frenzy of bloodlust. He marched against her now, but this army was nothing more than the first wave. If another was needed, it would come, and it would be larger. And likewise with the next, and the next after that. She could not win.

Yet she would fight anyway, and he felt a rush of admiration. He could show it to no one, but it was there, and his heart went out to her in pity. She had not asked for this, and if her forefather truly was the emperor, she had not asked for that either. Nor the prophecy. Even so, the world spun forward as it did, and whether she wanted any of it or not that was where she found herself.

Nomgar would care nothing for that though, nor understand that the same applied to him. He was where he was because of one of his ancestors, a man who had taken the chieftainship from another, supported by the shaman to do so. Argash knew the stories well, for the man it had been taken from was his own great grandfather, and though Nomgar was related to him, he felt little love there and no admiration. The man was a fat, pompous and incompetent moron. Skaaghul was another matter though. There was a mean streak in him, and a degree of rat-like cunning.

Argash let out a deep breath, and allowed himself a dangerous thought. Might not an emperor, swift of mind, vigorous, caring for the citizens, solve many of the problems that beset the Cheng nation and bring good to her people? Was not Shar such a person?

A dangerous thought indeed, and one Skaaghul would kill him for in an instant. If he ever knew of it.

Yet life was short anyway, and death was not the worst thing that could happen to a man. Perhaps it would be worth the risk to gauge if any others that he knew, in positions of leadership such as himself, felt the same way. He would risk his life doing that, so he must be careful. But if he thought that way, there would be others.

The army marched ahead, and Argash marched with it. His mind was elsewhere though, and his heart was troubled. For whom would he rather die? Nomgar, Skaaghul or Shar?

20. A Dark Current

Shulu wandered through the forest in a daze, and the stifling heat of the humid growth made it hard to breathe. At night, the chill of the cold stars pierced her to the bone, and she felt the world spin swiftly through the void.

"Here, drink of the nahaz," a voice said. It was Chen, and concern was in his eyes. "It will revive you and chase away the fever."

She went to drink, but the vision disappeared. Her son who could have been, the emperor that was, faded away. He was dead. He was gone long years ago, and she was alone. No one would care for her now.

There was Shar though. She would come! How uncanny it was that through the endless generations a descendant of the emperor would still look so much like him, be made of the same iron will and gentle soul.

No. Shar was elsewhere. She was in danger. She was hunted, and they would kill her if they could.

Hunted. Yes, she had been hunted too. She remembered spirit walking. Then Three Moon Mountain and the Conclave of the Shamans. Yes. Yes! She had set the fear of death upon them and broken them up. But she had been hunted in turn. They had pursued her to the cave, and near death she had fought them off and fled.

Near death. The words rang true in the silence of her mind. She stumbled over a root, and straightened slowly, using the tree as a support and shivering as she hugged it.

She had escaped, but she had grown sick. A fever racked her body, and she felt the sweat of sickness drip from her. There would be no nahaz here. She needed water though, and ahead was a forest stream. She heard it bubble through the shadows somewhere a little beyond her sight. Unless that were imagined too.

She stumbled toward it, fell, then crawled on her knees. At last she felt the coolness of it on her face, and she drank as a wild animal to quench her raging thirst. She looked about, suddenly wary, for her enemies were in the forest searching for her. She saw nothing though, and drank again. The whole stream would not be enough to satisfy her, but her belly was now full.

Standing up on shaky legs, she looked around. This was a brief moment of clarity, and she thought through her position. She must hide, for she could travel no farther. After that, fate would decide if her enemies found her or not, and if she lived or died.

She staggered upstream, looking for somewhere that offered concealment. She knew she was leaving tracks, but it could not be helped. The fever grew upon her again, and her vision swam. Dizzy, she fell once more to her knees. Yet doing so, she saw a dark cranny that might serve. It was above the waterline, but not by much. The root of some great tree that overshadowed the water bulged up from the earth, and beneath it was a hollow such as some beast might use for a den. She crawled into it, and curled up to shiver in her misery.

She could see the dark current of the stream sweep by below her, and it turned and tilted, eddying one way and then another. So it was with her memory, for again she was with the emperor in the great days of the Cheng nation. She loved him, and his death had nearly killed her. She felt the pain of it again, and hot tears streamed down her muddy face. She cried for Shar too, who had been assassinated by the shamans. Who was there now who would give her nahaz and care for her? None. All were dead.

A moment of clarity came to her again. Shar yet lived, and she, old and sick as she was, must survive to help her charge when she would need it most. Her trial of hardships was only just beginning, and the test of her character as a leader was but at the first step of a long journey.

What was needed now was sleep. Sleep would heal her, or else she would never wake and drift into the void, the hollow serving as her grave.

Time passed, and the void beckoned. Day and night chased each other over the world, and Shulu's dreams drifted on the twilight shadows like a scent through the forest's dark aisles.

She drifted up to consciousness but once, and heard the footsteps of men outside and coarse laughter. Yet the void pulled her under again, and she slept.

Her enemies did not find her, for it was dark and they did not see her tracks. She slept, and dreamed deep dreams undisturbed by the world. Then again she woke, and her mind was clear.

The fever had broken. She lived, yet knew that death had been close. This den nearly had been her grave, and few would have marked her passing or ever known where her body rested. Who would have mourned for her? She had no children. Too deep she had delved into the secrets of magic, and the powers that formed and substanced the universe had changed her. For everything there was a price, even as night followed day, and so it was with sorcery.

There was Shar though. She would have mourned, and she was as a daughter. Yet she was more too. She was the daughter of destiny, and the fate of a nation rested on her shoulders.

Shulu felt thirst again, but she did not move. The stream was close, but there was danger too. She remembered the footsteps, but it was not that. Those enemies had gone. There was something else. She felt it in her bones and the hair on the back of her neck stood up.

It was daylight outside. She peered out from beneath the tree root, but saw nothing. Yet it was there. Or if not there, coming. That was it. It was not a person, but a creature of magic. It was a thing of evil and she sensed it even as she could hear a noise in the distance.

She closed her eyes and freed her mind. It was no great magic, and not as dangerous as spirit walking, yet she cast some part of herself out over the forest in like fashion. She could not quite hear or see, but she could gain an impression of the world.

She found it. A beast it was. A hunter. Dark magic infused it, and evil drove it. Perhaps it was a denizen of the forest, but more likely it was summoned by sorcery from some otherworldly pit. She could sense the touch of a shaman upon it. And it was hunting for her. It had her scent, and she was not strong enough to fight it. Not now.

Her mind was hers again, but she was still weak. She did not have the strength to defeat it, nor the strength to flee. She must make a last stand and sell her life as dearly as she could.

She crawled out of the den, and looked for a good place to stand and fight. There were trees all around, so at least she could protect her back. Even as she chose one that would best suit her, she saw a fallen log nearby. It straddled the bank, and the rushing water lapped at it.

It was an omen. Luck was on her side, or mayhap a god favored her. She rushed down to the log. It was too large for her to lift, but she looked around and soon saw a dead branch, thick and still strong. She used it as a lever to shift the log.

Nothing happened, and the strain of the effort made her dizzy again. Quickly she went to the other side and used the branch as a tool to dig away at the mud that supported the log. It did not shift, but water oozed up under it. She kept going, working as swiftly as her ancient body would allow, and she drew on a touch of magic to strengthen her. Better to use what little she had on this than save it for a fight with the beast, for it would not be enough to win her that battle.

She went around to the other side again, and once more tried to lever it. Still, nothing happened, but then it moved a finger's width and a little more water flowed under it. She kept going, panting deeply with her effort, and cold sweat broke out under over her brow.

It moved again, and this time it did not stop. The rush of the current gripped it, and she clambered over the log. She lay upon it, and it nearly rolled, but she used the branch as a crude paddle and pushed herself out toward the center of the flow. There the waters took her quickly, and it was more steady than she thought. At times she used the branch to stabilize the log, at others to help keep it riding the swift current in the middle of the stream.

She still sensed the beast, but could not tell quite what it was. Yet when it found where she had lain under the root, it broke out into a frenzy of howls something like a wolf. It was a terrible sound, yet mixed with the note of triumph within it grew an increasing strain of stifled bloodlust. It had her scent, but not her. She pictured it casting about and trying to find where she had gone, but without success. It could not follow her over water.

The creature howled madly, and the sound of it filled the shadowy forest with fear. Then swift as it started it stopped. That, too, was eerie. Every shadow held menace now. Every nook and cranny of the forest was a lair of fear.

Shulu ignored it. Her mind was playing tricks on her. She had outwitted the beast, and the one who had sent it. For now, at least.

She hoped she would have such luck in the future. She would need it.

21. The Time of Swords

Shar studied the scout as he spoke. He was not a young man, but like all the scouts under Radatan's command, he was experienced. A hunter he might be back in the hills, but he also knew his business as a warrior.

"The enemy is ahead," he told her.

The sun was setting, and the last rays glinted over her army as they prepared for the evening meal.

"How long before we reach them?"

"It'd take several hours. If we leave at dawn, we should reach them before noon. Assuming they march toward us as well, which is likely, it will be midmorning."

The scout had dismounted from his pony, and the beast nickered as he scratched its ears. She understood the bond between them, for as a scout his life might depend on it, and it in turn depended on him.

"We'll see about that," she replied. Already a plan was forming in her mind. "How large is their force?"

"Not as large as we thought, emperor-to-be. But they outnumber us by about half as much."

In truth, Shar had expected more. Likely there were more on the way though, and this was just the closest tribes being her own Fen Wolves and the Soaring Eagles. That, too, informed the plan that was bubbling away in her mind.

"And the land between us?"

"All flat grasslands, just as it is here. There's no place of particular advantage."

Shar dismissed him, and he led his pony away. As all the scouts did, he would treat it well now, rubbing it down, watering it and giving it a good feed which would include some grain.

The decision of what to do was ultimately hers, but the chiefs were experienced and she respected their opinions, some more than others. It was best to consult them and get the benefit of that. Likewise, she did not wish to seem as though she ignored them. Their cooperation was important, and the last thing she needed now was disunity that could be avoided.

They gathered around for their evening meal, and she told them what the scout had said. Even as she spoke, another scout returned and reported the same information to them all.

"Well, what do you think?" she asked.

"Hit them hard tomorrow," Nahring replied. "If you wait and try to lure them to ground more favorable to you, whatever reinforcements they have will have that much more time to reach them."

That seemed to be the collective advice from them all, and Sagadar added to it. "Besides," he said, "there likely isn't favorable ground anywhere nearby. You could march for days and all you'll find is grassland."

She was pleased with these answers. The chiefs had the will to fight, even against a superior force. They reckoned their tough hill warriors were more hardened to battle. Life was hard in the hills, and small skirmishes between different tribes was common. It was that way all over the land, but in the hills the tribes were gathered in together over a smaller area so direct conflict was more common.

She nodded. "I'm pleased with you all. And this is our best chance. Hit them hard and soon. Defeat them before help arrives for them. But I can add one thing to the plan to maximize that and give us the upper hand."

Kubodin was grinning, and she thought he knew what she was going to propose. Asana glanced up at her, and if she could read his inscrutable face better these days, he knew as well.

"We'll start our march three hours before dawn. That way, we'll arrive and attack them at sunrise. They won't be ready for us. Even if they know where we are now, which is doubtful because we're capturing their scouts, they'll not expect that."

Kubodin grinned broadly now. "I like it! They have an advantage in numbers, but if that plan works we can negate it. And more."

Sagadar was not so convinced. "If it doesn't work, we'll be in trouble though. The men won't like marching in the dark, and they'll be deprived of sleep. If the enemy is ready for us, then it will be a slaughter."

Shar did not disagree. "There's an element of risk. As for sleep, the army will still get most of the night. They'll not be tired, and they'll know what a huge advantage this will be for us. I think they'll love the plan, when it's explained to them. It might save their lives. As for the enemy expecting us, I've given orders to escalate our own scouting operations. Few of the enemy scouts will get through to us, and if some do and return to give warning, they won't be far ahead of us."

It was a long night, and the midnight hour neared before Shar slept herself. She kept getting reports from the scouts, and all seemed good news. What troubled her though was the possibility of a spy in the camp. If word of her plan was already on the way to her enemies, then her tactic would indeed put them at greater risk. Yet against this, she had given orders. The ring of sentries around the camp was strong, and it worked two ways. It protected against the enemy, but they also had orders to let no one save scouts leave the camp. As for them she had to trust to Radatan's judgement. He had chosen them all.

At the appointed hour, the army began to march, and it was eerie for such a large force to move in the dark. It would also be a test of her commanders because keeping their forces together and not getting strung out would be difficult.

There was grumbling at first, but by the time they were moving the men were in good spirits. They trusted her, and they understood her ploy. If it worked, it was one that could bring them not only victory but leave many of them alive to enjoy it.

Shar set as fast a pace she could in the dark, and she sent word throughout the army to move with stealth from the halfway point onward. There would be no singing as they were want to do, or horns. Nothing would be allowed to give them away.

Enemy scouts were still the greatest danger. It only took one to observe their night march and report back to dull the surprise of it. Yet several had been captured, some while they slept for the night. They were not as efficient as her own, even if it turned out that some were leng-fah from her own tribe, but not from her old band. These were good scouts, but they were in country that was foreign to them. Nor did they expect her swift advance. It seemed, so far as interrogation of the captured enemy had revealed, that the scouts had only just been deployed. The enemy leadership had been lazy. Or had badly miscalculated her expected position.

Shar cast her gaze to the east, and saw the first graying of the sky. It made her nervous. She had come a long, long way since fleeing Tsarin Fen, but she might not live to see another dawn. This could be her last, and it seemed beautiful to her. The precious that might be lost was always more appreciated.

She studied her army now that the dim light revealed it. It was still in the right formation, and no one had lagged or separated during the march. So far, so good.

Radatan approached. "I've word from the scouts," he said.

"What is it?"

"More of the enemy were captured quite recently. Some were killed in a skirmish."

"And the enemy army?"

He grinned. "Apparently unaware of our approach. They're preparing for their breakfast."

Shar sniffed the air, and she detected a hint of smoke on it. The breeze, such as it was, did not bring it in her direction, but they were close enough that it could be smelled anyway.

"You've done well, Radatan. You and your scouts. Tell them they have my thanks, and they can fall back to the rear of the army. Stealth is at an end, and now the time of swords has come."

They moved ahead, and as the day dawned and the sun brightened, the enemy soon came into sight. At the same time, the enemy saw them and their scurry of activity was frantic.

"They're like a giant ant's nest that's just been kicked hard," Kubodin said.

"So they are. But ants can still bite."

Shar studied the ground between them as her army advanced. It was flat grassland as she had been told, yet there was an area of drier grass and rocks slightly to her left. She gave orders to move to the right of this. The rocks were ankle height at the tallest, and would provide little hindrance to either foot soldiers or cavalry, but it *would* be harder to traverse and she used it to help strengthen her left flank, if only marginally. The smallest things could make a difference.

Blood was about to be spilled. Cheng warriors were about to die, and it did not matter which side they were on. They were *all* Cheng, and Shar wanted to avoid that. She could try to talk to the enemy commanders, but that was futile. The swifter she attacked, and the faster she forced a surrender, the more warriors she could save.

Shar studied them as they hurried into position, campfires still burning as they hastened to gird swords and armor. The Soaring Eagle Tribe was at the left, and her own Fen Wolves to the right. There was a significant gap between the two tribes though, and the Fen Wolves were farther back too. They were like two separate forces rather than a single army, and apparently had marched as such. Some of the scouts had noted that, and she wondered exactly what it meant, and if she could exploit the lack of unity.

She had seen all she needed to see. Her tactic had worked, and there was nothing for it now but to fight, and the sooner the better. She glanced at Asana, stony faced but calm. If he had any advice, he would already have given it. She glanced at Kubodin. The little man tugged at his brass earring thoughtfully, but said nothing.

Radatan was waiting, a horn in his hands, and Huigar beside him. They would stick close to her now, and try to protect her as best they could. She did not intend to fight, but it could not be ruled out. If things went badly, she would need to.

Radatan was watching her closely, and she nodded grimly.

"Blow the horn."

He took it to his lips, and the sound of it rang loud and clear across the grasslands. The enemy heard it and looked up. They knew what it meant, and so did her own army. They swept forward in a trotting march, faster than walking but not a run. The whole army moved as one, its front like a battering ram that would crash into the enemy, and each flank curved back for protection. It was on those flanks also that she had deployed what few archers there were.

The army surged forward, and the tramp of their boots was as the tramp of doom. All that was yet to be decided was whose doom it was.

22. The Scream of Swords

Shar went ahead with the army, but she was toward the rear. She, and her command group that included Asana and the chiefs, had commandeered ponies so as to better see the battle and therefore control it.

The two forces met with a scream of swords. Men died, and blood wetted the earth. Shar tried to summon Stillness in the Storm, but it would not come.

All that was happening now was because of her. And the shamans. Guilt swamped her, and she regretted not trying to talk to the enemy first. What had happened to her? Was she becoming cold and heartless as the shamans? Was destiny squeezing the humanity from her like water from a wet cloth?

She was different than she had been, and that change had not yet run its full course. For good or for ill, fate was changing her. Yet she straightened. It had been a cold and hard decision to attack. Even so, her reasoning had been sound. It did not seem so, but in the end this would save more lives. At least, if her surprise had the desired effect and forced a surrender.

She rose up in the stirrups of her pony to better see. Her force was devastating the enemy, and driving forward. Even so, the Soaring Eagles were fighting back. They had been taken unawares, but every moment that passed now they were shoring their ranks up and beginning a fierce resistance. It was not a good sign.

She looked to the right, and saw that the Fen Wolves were separating themselves farther from the Soaring

Eagles and swinging around to face her right flank. But they had not yet joined the fray.

"What are *they* doing?" she asked.

The others were looking too. "Perhaps they're just being held in reserve," Sagadar suggested.

Kubodin scratched his head. "If they're being held in reserve, why maneuver like that? Why show us where they're going to attack from and warn us, but not actually attack?"

Shar could think of another possibility. "Perhaps they're supposed to have attacked already, but something is holding them back. Disunity maybe. Or a reluctance to fight alongside a clan that has been their enemy." She glanced at Asana. "What do you think?"

The swordmaster, also standing in his stirrups but doing it more gracefully than the others, studied the Fen Wolves closely.

"Impossible to say. It could be all those things, or something else. But you must, at the least, assume they'll attack eventually."

They still showed no sign of doing so, but she knew Asana was right. She must assume they would, and if not now then soon. They might be waiting until her army tired and used its own reserves to fight on the front line. At that point, the Fen Wolves could press in against her side and engage her tired troops with fresh ones.

She decided to take a risk. That flank could be left as it was, and she would wait and see. Her right wing was there, and it could peel back quickly and offer protection. She would not be caught off guard.

The others noted that she gave no orders for a change in position, and Asana raised an eyebrow but said nothing. The fighting on the front line was growing even fiercer, and she turned her attention back to that for the moment.

Death screams filled the air, and the Soaring Eagles had now stopped the slow advance forward. They were losing more men than she was, but they had more to start with. From behind their forces a group of reserves detached themselves, and moved around to her left flank.

Shar watched them but a moment, and made an instant decision. She signaled Radatan, and he blew several notes on his horn.

Instantly the left wing of her army extended so as to cover the entire left flank. It was a thin phalanx, being only three lines deep. It would have to do though. There were no other forces to support them.

"They seek to use their greater numbers against us," Asana said.

"So they do. It might work, but I think they'll have a hard time of it there."

Shar glanced to the right flank. Still the Fen Wolves did not attack. She looked back the left, and watched patiently.

There was some skirmishing with archers. Both sides had some, but neither many. It was a situation she must remedy, and swiftly.

The Soaring Eagles phalanx approached, shields high and trotting in. But Shar had positioned her left wing well. The rocky ground there was hindering the enemy, and it allowed more time for the few archers her force had to kill them. This was made easier as the uneven ground caused the approaching men to raise and lower their shields as they stumbled.

The sky suddenly filled with spears, a favorite weapon of the Smoking Eyes and Green Hornet tribes, though the spears of the Green Hornets were more slender, and likely the tips were poisoned. More of the enemy went down. Then the two forces met in a crash of shields and wild yelling.

Shar felt her legs tremble. This was a turning point of the battle. If her wing broke here, she must call a retreat. Or else go thither and fight herself. Her presence might be enough to hold the line. Perhaps. But then she must leave command of the overall battle to another, and as much as she admired Kubodin and Asana, she did not wish to do that. The responsibility was hers alone.

A quick glance to her right told her that still nothing was happening there, and she swung around to the left again.

She waited silently, but her heart pounded in her chest. So much depended on what would happen next. Her entire lifetime had been hurtling toward this moment, and all that she had ever done, or ever could be, had come to a crossroads.

Slowly, it became apparent that the left wing was holding. Relief began to flow through her, and she felt the tension that had been in all those around her start to ease as well.

She took her gaze off the left wing and focused on the main battle at the front. It was touch and go there. Her line was holding though, but it would not take much for either side to gain an advantage. When that happened, momentum would be with whoever had it, and the other side must give way. The moment that happened, the tide of the battle had turned and it would be doubly hard, if not impossible, to turn it back.

Shar felt that emotionless cold come over her that often did at times of her greatest testing. She had cast herself into the currents of fate, as all must who tried to become great leaders. Destiny chose the outcome though, not themselves. They were at its mercy, and like a game of dice must abide the results of seeming chance. The failures were forgotten, and their names buried beneath the weight of years. The successful earned fame in their lifetime, and the tale of years would keep telling their story after they had passed to dust. Yet all, all of them, faced this same crossroads and took this same chance.

The fate of the empire rested on destiny. Or as others called it, luck. Shar felt that luck was always on her side though. Even when things went wrong for her, they were proved to be a boon in the end.

"Mistress!" Radatan called, interrupting her thoughts.

"What is it?"

He pointed to the right flank. "Look at the enemy messengers."

She did so. There were several going in each direction, from the Soaring Eagles to the Fen Wolves, and back the other way. They rode ponies, probably those that belonged to the scouts now that there was no need for scouting.

"There seem to be a lot of them," Shar said.

"I've been watching them for a while," Radatan replied. "There are more now, but they've been racing back and forth for a while."

"Well spotted, Radatan." She looked around at everyone. "What interpretation do you put on it?"

"It might mean the Fen Wolves were supposed to attack, but haven't. And the Soaring Eagles want to know why," Nahring said.

"Maybe," Asana agreed. "There's no way to know though. They might also just be refining their plan, and determining the best time for an all-out assault."

Shar knew both interpretations could easily be right. Even so, the Fen Wolves were her own tribe, and they must know she led this army. She hoped that might have something to do with it.

It was time to act. The battle was poised evenly just now, and she must try to throw the dice in her favor. For that, she had a plan.

"Huigar," she said. "You have the banner that was made earlier. Ride out to the right flank, and unfurl it when you get there. Ride up and down the outside of the wing a few times."

Her guard galloped off straight away, and Kubodin looked at her with narrow eyes.

"What trick is this?" he asked. "What do you expect the banner to do?"

"Watch and see," she replied.

23. Attack!

The tribes of the Cheng did not use banners, but they knew what they were. The great emperor had used one, and on those times when rulers from other nations visited they often displayed theirs.

Huigar reached the outside of the wing, and there she drew her pony to a halt. She knew all eyes were upon her, including her father. Nahring was near to Shar, and he would not show it but he would certainly feel pride that she had been chosen for this.

Slowly, drawing the moment out, she unfurled the banner. It was attached to a spear, and when the cloth was loosed from the cords that bound it, she raised it high in one hand.

The air was still, and no breeze caught it. But then she nudged her pony forward into a trot and the banner played out in the wind of its passing. In its center was a wolf, and not just any wolf but a fen wolf. Shar's tribe would recognize the slight differences in the leaner body and the longer ears. It was Shar's acknowledgment of respect to her origins and the clan that had nurtured her. It also said to that clan that she respected and honored them for doing so. And, it might be, it would trigger a sense of returned loyalty to her.

Yet Shar was above the clans now, belonging not to one but to all as an emperor must. The background to the wolf was a field of green, for most of the Cheng nation was comprised of grassland. And behind the wolf, as though in the distance, was a chain of snow-capped mountains. These represented the Eagle Claw Mountains that were like the backbone running through the length of the Cheng nation.

Drubadar felt blood trickle down his side. The Soaring Eagle warrior before him had managed to get past his shield and strike him with the edge of his sword. It was not a bad wound, but a few inches higher and it would have taken him near the armpit and he would no longer be able to hold the shield to defend himself. Or more toward the center and it might have slipped through his ribs and killed him.

All he wanted to do was swear and curse, and then kill the warrior in front of him before the man could do the same to him. This was not his first battle though. If he lived he could curse all he wanted, but if he did he knew he would feel a rush of joy amid all the death instead at just surviving. For now, he must remain patient and wait his chance.

He stabbed out, and the other man deflected the blow with his own shield. That done, the man hammered his sword at Drubadar's shield, which was duly fended off in turn. So the contest went, just as it did up and down the entire length of the line.

Here and there a warrior fell on either side, and a scream from the wounded man was cut short as a slashed throat ended the life of whoever it was. The ground was slick with blood, and the stench of entrails and urine was in the air. He ignored it. To think of that was to unman himself. So at least his father had told him when he first learned to wield a sword as a child. *Fight your own battle, lad. You're not the army. Win your own struggle with patience, and let your warrior brothers win their own in turn. When enough of you do that, you win the battle.*

Drubadar suddenly thought his father had been wise. He thought only of the man before him, and went through the motions of defend and attack. Waiting.

His chance came, for his opponent, perhaps growing tired, tried to hit even harder with a great overhead strike and finish this contest off. It nearly worked, for though Drubadar managed to raise his shield high enough in time to fend off the blow, the weight of it buckled his knees. Yet this gave him an opportunity. His sword arm was lower, and his opponent stumbled slightly delivering the strike, and his shield moved a little to the side.

There was a gap in his enemy's defenses, and Drubadar took it. The tip of his blade darted forward like a snake striking, and it plunged past shield and sword and through the leather jerkin deep into the man's lower belly. He reeled back, his guts spilling out as he stumbled away and he was lost in the crowd behind as a new foe took his place.

This man was fresh, and he was huge. Drubadar knew that no patience would win this battle. He was going to die.

The first blow nearly did it. It was a fast jab at his neck, and he only just managed to raise his shield in time. Even so, it was only the rim that deflected it, so the tip slid past close to his neck and on the way back the edge cut his skin.

With a grunt, the huge man bashed his shield into Drubadar's and tried to press him back. Drubadar resisted, but he stepped back once, and then a second time. In doing so he twisted a little to the side. His opponent turned to follow him, and exposed his side to the next man in line beside Drubadar.

The big man had been assured of victory, but even so cold steel slipped between his ribs and killed him. He toppled down, and Drubadar glanced at the man who had saved him.

It was Rackgar, the boy who had grown up on the farm across the road from him. They had learned to hunt together, and to fight together, but had never liked each other.

"Thanks!" Drubadar yelled above the din.

"We're going to win this!" the other man called back.

Drubadar was not so sure. Another enemy was moving in on him, but even as he prepared for that he saw a small axe hurtle through the air from someone farther back in the ranks. There was a loud crack, and it struck him in the head.

He fell back, and found himself looking up at the sky. He could feel no pain, but he could not seem to move. His vision changed though, and a black circle seemed to form around each eye, and it contracted until all that was left were two pinpricks of blue light. Then even that was gone.

Despite the lack of pain, he knew he was dying, or already dead. He tried to think of why, but it meant nothing to him if an emperor ruled or the shamans. He had been told to fight by his chief, so he fought. That was all.

He dreamed of his childhood, and saw the dusty lane leading to the hut where he was born and the goats in the fields about him. *Father? Father? Where are you?* he called out. There was no answer, and then even the farm was gone and there was nothing.

Argash was troubled, for his life was in jeopardy. He had faced death several times before though, and it did not stop him from doing what was right. He was not sure if what he was doing was right or wrong, though.

"I order you to attack!" Nomgar was screaming at him, and Argash had never seen his chief so angry. There was a froth of foam in the corners of his lips, and his eyes were wild.

"I will not," Argash replied. Even as he answered he saw the guard of nazram around the chief advance toward him. He was not surprised. Refusing to attack had been treason, but all along the line other captains had made the same choice. He had been the first though, and somehow the chief had learned that he had conspired with the others.

His hand fell to his sword hilt, ready to draw and defend himself to the death. He did not have to though. All around him warriors stepped forward, and they outnumbered the nazram and faced them down.

Argash sent a prayer of thanks to the gods. But this was not over. What would have happened next, he did not know, for at just that moment a cry went up from the ranks and several arms pointed.

He looked out toward Shar's army. It was holding its ground well, which had helped him convince some of the other captains not to attack. They did not wish to die, but it was not the cause of the excitement.

There was a rider there, and even as he watched the figure nudged their pony forward and a banner such as the stories of old often mentioned unfurled. The first thing he saw was the wolf, and his blood stirred.

"I'll not attack," he told the chief quietly. "That's Shar out there in that army somewhere. It's her army, but she's one of us. She's a Fen Wolf, and no enemy of ours."

"Then you'll die!" screamed Nomgar.

Shar felt a surge of pride. Her army was holding up against the enemy, and the banner sent a shiver of emotion through her. The fen wolf was her totem animal, and she felt a love of her old home sweep through her. At the same time, the banner represented all the Cheng, and so many of them were here fighting together as a single entity for a single cause. There was reason to hope that they might prevail against the shamans and grow into the strong nation they deserved to be, rather than subdued as clans that bickered amongst each other while the shamans ruled and stole the wealth of the land.

The emotion faded and that cold and clear mind gripped her that always did at the pivotal moments of her life. Now, she must act and win this battle. Or die trying to.

24. Sorcery Unleashed

Shar told Radatan to blow seven short notes on his horn. It was a prearranged signal to the general who led a group of Smoking Eyes and Green Hornet warriors at the rear of the left wing.

Once more Shar stood in her stirrups and watched. The general did not waste any time. He and his men, only a hundred strong, swept out beyond the wing and faced the flank of the force attacking that side of Shar's army.

When the warriors were in position, they loosed a volley of arrows. High the shafts arced into the air, and then they plummeted as a deadly rain. It was an unexpected maneuver, for once engaged in battle the Cheng rarely resorted to archers, and they had few of them anyway.

The archers were well skilled with their bows. Many of the arrows were deflected by shields, but many were not. Soaring Eagle tribesmen died, and quite a few were injured. Confusion broke out, and those fighting in the very first line sensed the chaos behind them and this drained their morale.

Again and again the archers loosed their arrows, and the confusion became greater. Shar saw that the Soaring Eagle commander on that flank had signaled for his own archers to come around from the rear of his force and return the hail of arrows. Shar had been waiting for this. Again she told Radatan to blow his horn.

Radatan blew two long notes, and then a third sharp one. It was the command for the left wing to advance. This they did, sensing the confusion the enemy was suffering and that their attention had faltered from the battle to the deadly skirmish on the side.

Shar watched, and Kubodin grinned widely. "That's a good man in charge of those archers," he said. "He got them into exactly the right place, and he used them well."

It was true, and Shar agreed. An emperor could lead an army, but it was wasted effort if her commanders could not put her plans into action exactly as discussed, and swiftly. The general had done both.

The left wing began to roll forward. It was slow at first, but that did not last long. Under assault from archers, and pressed hard by the infantry, the attacking force of the Soaring Eagles wilted. They began to retreat in disarray, and the enemy archers were caught up in the confusion and could do nothing except retreat as well.

Shar studied the right wing. Still, there was no sign of attack from the Fen Wolves. But they were there like a thundercloud that might break into wind and rain at any time, or fade away to nothing.

The front of her army was fighting hard, and there were signs that the confusion of the enemy's flanking maneuver was observed by both sides there. Her warriors were fighting harder, and the enemy were anxious.

"It's time to try to break them," Shar said. "Do you agree?"

The chiefs around her nodded, but she paid most attention to Kubodin and Asana.

"Do it," the little hill man said.

"It's time," Asana agreed.

Shar turned one more time to Radatan. "Signal for the front line to advance," she called.

Radatan did so, and he blew lustily on the horn. This time it was one long note to designate the front ranks of the army, and a single sharp one that meant to press forward.

The front line responded instantly. It was obvious though that the enemy were going to put up a harder fight here. They were not suffering the attack from archers that the enemy on the left flank had done.

On the right side of the front, a large group of Iron Dogs fought. They did not move swiftly, but they seemed relentless in their push forward. The line of the enemy buckled before them, and the Iron Dogs pressed onward.

"Not too deep," whispered Dakashul.

Shar saw the risk too. If they penetrated too far into the enemy ranks, they could be cut off from the rest of their line, surrounded and killed.

The fighting was fierce, and just when Shar thought they were going to make the error she feared, whoever commanded them must have given a signal to his men. They advanced no more, but held their ground.

"Good man!" Dakashul said with a tight smile.

"Look at the rest of the line," Asana added.

Shar saw what he meant. The rest of the front line was pushing forward, and they were slowly drawing level with the Iron Dogs. The Iron Dogs, seeing this, pressed forward again themselves. Shar felt the spirits of those around her rise. This was it. This was the moment victory could be theirs.

The shamans had other ideas. In defiance of convention, they began to use their sorcery against the Iron Dogs. It was unthinkable that they did so, but it was equally unthinkable to them that they should lose this battle.

From behind the enemy ranks, where the shamans stood together, they lofted balls of fire high into the air. The fire burned with eldritch light, multihued and swirling from one color to another.

The sorcerous attacks fell from the sky into the Iron Dogs, and a number of warriors fell instantly, yet others burned alive.

They were brave men though, those who had been struck and those who fought by their side and did not flee. Even on fire, they ran into the ranks of the enemy, laying about them with their gleaming swords. Their comrades, who must have wished to retreat, uttered a great battle cry instead and renewed their attack.

Shar felt sick. No man should die as these were, and sorcery might yet turn the battle. No army could long endure this.

"This will kill us all," Sagadar said.

He was right. No matter how brave her army, sooner or later this would be too much. Sorcery came at a cost though, and the two shamans doing this must tire. But if that did not happen soon, it would make no difference.

Shar knew what must be done. "Asana. You have the command."

She gave that order loudly so that all the chiefs might hear her. They respected the swordmaster, and would obey him. Especially given that he was not a chief from among their own order that had been set above them.

"Kubodin, if you are willing, come with me. Those two shamans need killing, and only you and I have enchanted weapons that can stand against their sorcery."

"I'm willing," Kubodin answered, and there was a look of terrible anticipation in his glance. The shamans might have made a mistake in using sorcery against warriors if that look was any indication. It might win them the battle, but it would also gain them the enmity of the people. Kubodin seemed fit to strangle them with his bare hands if he could, and she did not blame him.

They kicked their ponies into a gallop, and headed to the right flank. Speed was the only thing that would serve them, for they must circle around behind the enemy and kill the shamans there. It was a mission that could only end in death, for if the shamans did not kill them, then the enemy army would. The only chance they had was to get there before anyone realized what they were doing, kill the shamans, and then swiftly flee. If that could be called a chance at all.

Their ponies raced ahead, and Kubodin was bent low over the back of his. Shar matched him for speed, but heard another pony close behind.

Looking over her shoulder, she saw Radatan bent low over the neck of his galloping pony, intent on catching up to them.

"Go back!" she yelled. "You have no magic. You'll die where we go!"

The hunter yelled back at her. "Mistress! I'm your bodyguard. Where you go I go!"

Shar's pony stumbled and then righted itself. She bent low over it again, and let it have its head. She could not dissuade Radatan, but she feared for his life. Yet it was his choice to make. She could not make him her bodyguard and then dishonor him by stopping him from carrying out his duty.

They turned the corner around the flank of her battling army and then raced along the right side toward the enemy. Radatan drew level with her and Kubodin, coming around the corner on the inside. Then suddenly Huigar was racing with them as well.

Shar thought of trying to send the woman back, but she had no more right to deny her than she did Radatan. At least the hunter knew the risks though. Yet surely Huigar must have realized what was happening and what their urgent mission was. The sorcerous fire still rained down upon the army from the Wahlum Hills, and Huigar knew that Shar carried the legendary swords of the emperor that were infused with magic. She must guess their deadly task.

They raced ahead, and Shar glanced to her right. The army of the Fen Wolves was still there, neither advancing nor retreating. What they would do, she could not guess. If they attacked though, Asana would take steps.

Shar felt that coldness clutch her again as it always did. This was madness, and she would die. Yet that fear was remote from her, as though it belonged to someone else. All that mattered was that this had to be done, and she and Kubodin were the only ones who could do it.

To her left, the flank of the enemy army was exposed. She saw warriors looking at her, but no one took steps. A handful of riders was not to be feared, and perhaps they even thought they were messengers from the Fen Wolves.

Shar glanced over at Huigar, and saw that her guard still carried the spear, but the banner was wrapped around it. That was a relief, otherwise she was announcing who they were.

Another flash of sorcerous light sizzled through the air and fell upon the front rank of Shar's army. With a wild yell Kubodin took the corner, and Shar was right beside him but silent. They were now at the rear of the enemy, and some way ahead she saw the two shamans. There was a small group with them, probably the chiefs and senior advisers, and there were nazram too. Yet they faced ahead, intent on the magic that was being invoked and the damage it was doing to Shar's army.

The ponies raced ahead, and it seemed that the grass swept below them as though it were the wind. It was not fast enough for Shar though. Here were two of her great enemies, and against all convention and rules of decency, they cast magic at flesh and blood warriors who could not defend against it. She would destroy them, and out of her emotionless cold a burning anger began to rise. She would kill these shamans even if it cost her everything.

The shamans were intent upon their sorcery, and they did not see the riders approach. Shar leaped off her pony even as it ran, for she would need to use her twin swords. Kubodin did the same near her, the wicked-looking axe of his ancestors in his hand.

"Behind you!" warned some of the nazram that at last had seen Shar approach, or at least realized it was an enemy attack.

Radatan and Huigar did not dismount. Instead, they charged directly into the nazram and laid about them with their swords, but it was the ponies and their flying hooves and thundering gallop that caused the most confusion.

Shar had no time to watch her guards. The shamans turned and faced her, fire dripping from their fingers as the sorcery in them built toward another attack.

She recognized Skaaghul, the shaman of the Fen Wolves. He was old, and even fatter than when she had last seen him. His white hair was plastered to his skull, and sweat was on his brow. Shulu had said he had little magic, but that was compared to her. To Shar, he might be dangerous enough to kill her despite her swords. It was clear that he recognized her too, for his eyes widened in surprise and then his face flushed with anger.

The other shaman she did not know, and he looked younger and stronger. He was also the first to react, and his hands darted forward sending a burst of sorcerous flame at her.

The flame hurtled at her, but she stood her ground. Legs fixed to the earth like trees, she braced herself and crossed the Swords of Dawn and Dusk before her body. Even so, the shock of the blast was greater than she expected. This man was more powerful than the shamans of the Two Ravens and Green Hornet clans that she had defeated before.

Shar staggered back, then fell. Sorcerous fire sprayed away from the swords, but she was alive and came to her feet running.

To her side there was a thunderous crash as Skaaghul attacked Kubodin. She dared not even glance in his direction to see if her friend still lived. All that mattered was reaching the shaman before he attacked again.

She could not. Again he raised his hands, but this time he struck with one only, hurtling flame toward her as though he scooped it out of the air and threw it like a spear.

Once more she stood her ground, and the swords caught the sorcery. She kept her balance, for the force was lesser this time, and she tilted the blades forward. The fire gathered on the blades, swirling in a dark mass, and then arced back toward the Soaring Eagle shaman.

Never had she seen a shaman move so quick, but her enemy dived and rolled like a warrior, came to his feet and raised his hands again. He would not be easy to kill.

The sorcery arced off her swords and leaped into the back ranks of the Soaring Eagle army. She had not planned that, yet warriors fell in writhing flames and chaos ensued. It was not intended, but it would help her cause.

She was running once more, and her foe was close now. Yet still he struck again. This time she dived and rolled herself, coming up beneath a spray of fire that would have killed her. It flared and then vanished, but the shaman was already moving. He tried to turn and flee into the ranks of his clan, but she was upon him and unleashed her fury.

Her first sword cut ran across the man's back. His tunic was torn, and an arc of blood showed. The man yelled, and turned to face her, fire growing at his fingertips.

She was too fast. Her other sword swept out, and his hand was severed. Crimson blood spurted, and a ghost hand of swirling magic seethed uncontrolled before her. She ignored it, driving both blades into the shaman's body.

Sorcery erupted from him in his death throes, flinging Shar away before she could withdraw the swords. She came to her feet, dizzy and disorientated. Her side stung, and she realized her clothes were smoldering. She rolled on the ground to put out whatever flame there was, then came up again.

A little way to her left, light flared and Skaaghul flung multihued flame at Kubodin. The little man did not dodge it. Rather he raised his axe and brought it down in a mighty stroke. It split the stream of fire in two, and a slow rumble filled the air as though thunder coursed through the skies.

Shar acted. There was no time to retrieve her swords. She leaped at Skaaghul, knocking him down and twining her arm around his neck as they fell. They hit the ground with a thud, and her grip tightened while fire flared at his hands. She saw the desire to kill her in his eyes, which were close to her own, but there was fear there also. As well there might be.

This was the man who had ordered her death even before it was known that she was descended from Chen Fei. He would receive no mercy from her, and the rage that had boiled through her before unleashed. With a mighty heave she wrenched her arm and twisted her body. There was a sickening crack, and Skaaghul went limp. He was dead.

"Quickly!" Kubodin yelled, and she saw why. Radatan and Huigar still lived, but they were fighting a losing battle against a number of nazram. They were still on their ponies though, and that was what had given them the ability to engage a greater number of warriors.

Shar ran back to claim her swords from the body of the shaman, and found that he was still alive. He could not move, but his eyes flickered open.

"We will beat you in the end," he whispered, blood frothing his lips. "We will kill you as we killed your forefather."

She did not answer him, but withdrew the swords. He convulsed, then lay still. The words could be taken as a mere curse, or a prophecy. She wondered if the dying words of her forefather had been any different.

Rising, she cast around for her pony. It had pulled up after she dismounted, and it was only fifty feet away, the reins trailing to the ground. She ran toward it, then slowed so as to be sure not to scare it away.

Kubodin was clambering atop his own pony, and she joined him and then swung around to her guards.

"To me!" she called. "To me!"

Radatan and Huigar disengaged with the nazram and galloped toward them. The hunter was wounded on his left arm, and Huigar was bleeding profusely from a cut above her eye. There seemed a lot of blood, but face wounds were like that. She seemed to sit well balanced on her horse, so hopefully it was a cut only and nothing more serious.

The nazram hesitated, not following for they could not hope to pursue them on foot, but not returning to the army either. Shar could see why. The enemy army was in chaos, for the blast of sorcery must have made them fear an attack from the rear.

"Unfurl the banner!" Shar yelled. If they feared an attack at the rear, the banner of their enemy there would fuel that thought further.

It seemed to be the last straw for the Soaring Eagles. They broke into a run, many discarding their weapons, and they fled the field to Shar's right, and away from their allies the Fen Wolves. The Fen Wolves remained where they were though, and they were still a formidable sized army, and fresh, whereas Shar's had just fought a battle.

"What will they do?" Kubodin asked.

Shar gave no answer. She did not know.

25. Brothers in Arms

Asana was now in charge of her army, but he did as Shar would have done. He pursued the retreating Soaring Eagles and harassed them.

"They at least aren't moving," Radatan said, pointing over at the Fen Wolf army.

"If they were going to attack, they would have done it by now," Shar replied.

She could not be sure of that, but nothing else made much sense. At any rate, if they did Asana had already deployed a phalanx to the rear to protect the army and he would disengage the pursuit of the Soaring Eagles. Even so, Shar itched to get back in control. She patted her pony's neck, and then nudged it forward in a gallop across the area where the enemy army had stood. Her own was ahead.

Huigar still flew the banner so they were recognized when they came near, and they raced to where Asana sat upon his horse directing the harassment of the enemy. When he saw her, he grinned broadly in a rare show of emotion.

"You beat the shamans!" he said. "And just as well. We couldn't have endured much more of their sorcery."

Surprisingly, he then reached out and clasped Kubodin's hand in the warrior's grip and shook it firmly. He might have showed little emotion, and tried his best to ride the highs and lows of life with tranquil acceptance, but there were times when emotion governed him despite that.

Nahring also nudged his horse close to Huigar's and hugged her.

"You did well, daughter,"

She flushed at that, but Shar agreed. "You did, and so did you Radatan."

"Look over there," Sagadar interrupted.

The Soaring Eagles were surrendering. Many of them threw down their weapons, and while others would have fought their situation was now hopeless. There was no point.

Shar approached, and she gave orders that all fighting was to cease. The surrender was accepted.

A hush fell over the field, broken only by the cawing of crows that had begun to gather. It was a sound familiar to the ears of all warriors, and too much had it been heard where tribes skirmished with other tribes. Shar was determined to prevent that in the future, and she knew that only the Cheng coming together as a single nation would do so.

She spoke to several warriors nearby. "Send word into the ranks of the Soaring Eagles. Tell them that I, Shar Fei, speak directly to them. They fought honorably today, even if the shamans did not. I hold nothing against them, and they will be able to march from here as free men, with their weapons, so long as they swear not to turn them against my army."

She asked if her messengers had committed that to memory, and when they had she added more to it.

"Tell them that today we were enemies, but that tomorrow we may fight as brothers. Tell them that their shaman and chief led them to this battle, which many others did not wish. For their sins against the Cheng nation that could be, I will judge them. Their shaman is already dead, killed by my own hand. Their chief must be sent to her so that he also may be judged."

She asked again if the messengers had committed this to memory, and when she was satisfied they had she added one more thing.

"Bring to me also the warrior known as Tarok, who once met with me, Asana and Kubodin on the grasslands of his clan as we were pursued by nazram, if he yet lives. I would speak with him."

The messengers left, and a camp was established. All the while the Fen Wolves remained where they were, and Shar ordered a message sent to them also. She asked for the chief Nomgar to submit himself to her judgement, and for the leng-fah captain Argash. Unless the Fen Wolves intended war, in which case she would fight them, but her heart did not wish that.

Her army was busy. They kept a phalanx active in case the Fen Wolves attacked, but otherwise established sentries, tended to the wounded and began the enormous task of burying the dead. She would not allow even the bodies of the enemy to remain as a feast for the crows, and there was not enough timber on the grasslands to fire the massive biers that otherwise would have been used.

A fire was lit though where some food could be prepared for her leadership group, and water boiled to clean and bandage their wounds.

It was not long though before a group of Iron Dog warriors returned with two men in their charge. One Shar knew. It was Tarok, and she was glad that he had survived the battle. The other was a formal looking man. He disdained to look at what he would take to be his captors, and looked at her instead, holding her gaze. He had the look of a warrior about him, and though he must guess he faced death he stood proudly before her.

"What is your name and title," Shar asked him.

The man studied her a moment, then answered in a matter-of-fact voice.

"I'm Lasalath, chief of the Soaring Eagles."

Shar returned his gaze steadily, and she gave an opportunity for her violet eyes to affect him as they usually did with others.

"Why did you fight me?" she asked.

At this, he looked away, but he did not look down. "I did my duty. The shaman ordered me to fight, and so I fought. What else would you expect of a chief but that he fulfills his responsibility?"

Shar was not going to play the game of answering his questions. She was in the position of authority, and the questions were hers to ask.

"Do you regret doing so?"

At that, some of his pride left him and his shoulders dropped slightly.

"I regret that there are so many dead."

Shar thought she understood him. It was hard to throw off the shackles of the shamans, and he had simply obeyed orders. He may not necessarily believe in her and what she could do, but if he were dead that would never change. Mercy and forgiveness might give him that opportunity. Moreover, showing such to those who had surrendered would send the right message in the future conflicts she would have. It could save lives in the days ahead.

"This then is my judgement," she said. "I strip you of the chieftainship of your clan. However, I declare you a free man, and a warrior of your tribe worthy of respect. You may leave freely, or stay with them. But know that they *will* join my army."

He seemed surprised by that, and she realized he had assumed he would be killed.

"There is one more thing," she continued. "I will appoint a chief in your place. He will be of your own tribe, and respected by your people. You are a free man, and you are free to dislike him, if you choose. Yet if you seek to undermine him I will have you executed. Do you understand?"

"I understand." His response was curt, for surely he would not like this, but at the same time he could not expect anything different.

Shar turned to Tarok. "It seems long ago that we met, yet by the count of days it is not. I'm glad you survived this battle."

Tarok offered her a bow. "The days have been relatively few, yet the change in your circumstances is great. Back then, I helped a questor for the swords. Now I see that you have not just found them, but are positioned as Nakatath, the emperor to be."

Shar was pleased. This man was as she remembered him, and he had not missed the opportunity to subtly suggest that he supported her. Nakatath was a word never used these days, but it was still remembered in the old stories. At least the few that survived that the shamans had not managed to suppress. It showed he was not just a warrior but also a man of cunning thought. He must guess why he had been asked here.

"The world hurtles forward," Shar replied, "and destiny unfolds before our eyes. I thank you for your help in the past, and I ask it again for the future. I offer you the chieftainship of the Soaring Eagle Clan, and that you join my army."

Tarok bowed again, but she studied his face closely and saw that there was no surprise there. He *had* guessed, and this confirmed her choice. A chief needed to see which way the winds were blowing.

"I accept," he answered. "I swear my allegiance to you, and I am proud to do so. Likewise, the Soaring Eagles will join your army." He surprised Shar by continuing. "And I thank you for your wise judgement with Lasalath, and if he is willing I would seek his counsel in the days ahead."

The former chief seemed surprised, but he gave a curt nod.

Shar thought it was a dangerous idea, for close to the seat of power in the clan the former chief might seek, and have the means, to try to regain his position. At the same time, the respect Shar had treated him with and now Tarok in turn would help bind the clan together. No doubt, there were still some who supported the shamans but this would make it harder for them to agitate strife.

"So be it," she said solemnly.

It was not long before another group arrived. Argash was among them, and her heart leaped at the sight of not just a Fen Wolf, but a man who had once been a friend. Nomgar was there also, and the man who had once been her chief did not look happy. His face was flushed, and a bruise was swelling over one eye. He had been struck, but she did not think any of her warriors had done it. The bruise would not have shown so soon. This was a blow from earlier, and by one of the chief's own people. She looked straight to Argash's knuckles, but saw no sign that he had done it. Even so, the enmity between the two men was plain.

"Hail, Nomgar, chief of my youth," Shar said.

Nomgar gave no reply save to spit toward her.

She studied him a long moment, showing no sign of emotion.

"Have you no greeting for your emperor-to-be?"

The man's face flushed red with anger. "A curse upon you! I will never bow to an upstart such as you. But the shamans will kill you before your army grows bigger."

Shar made her decision, and she made it swiftly. Here was a man who would work to fulfill the will of the shamans, and to thwart all she strove for.

"The shamans have tried to kill me. Again and again. Yet they are the ones dying. As will you. For your crimes against the Cheng people, and for your crimes against me, I condemn you to death. You will be hanged within the hour."

She signaled some warriors from around her. "Make it so. Do it quickly, but allow him to pray to whatever gods he reveres, if any."

Nomgar's mouth worked silently, froth building in the corners. After a moment, he found his voice.

"I am your chief! I command that *you* be hanged!"

She did not reply. The man had gone mad, and she guessed that he was always so, but the refusal of his warriors to join the battle, for such must have happened, had perhaps pushed him over an edge.

Nomgar was removed, and Shar turned her attention to Argash.

"Was it you that hit him?"

Argash had been watching his chief taken away, screaming and struggling with his guards.

"He drew a sword against me, so I disarmed him."

"Well that you did, and I perceive that you did much more."

Argash nodded gravely. "You guess well, as you always did."

"May my judgement be as good as my guesses. In you, I see a strong leader of the Fen Wolves. The chieftainship isn't foreign to your family as your great grandfather once led the clan. So, before these witnesses, in thanks for what you have done but more because of your abilities, I offer you the rule of the Fen Wolf Clan."

Argash seemed surprised, and he opened his mouth a few times as if to speak, but he could not gather his thoughts. At least it seemed so, but he may have been hiding that he had anticipated this. After a moment, he replied.

"You honor me greatly, emperor-to-be. I accept."

Shar clapped her hands. "Then it is done. Let there be a celebration throughout the army, and let us remember also those who have died."

She spoke to the chiefs then. "Let them celebrate victory, but we must plan for the future, and swiftly."

A clearing was made and a fire built. The hill tribes liked to hold their councils with the scent of smoke in the air, for according to their ways that was the breath of the gods and it imparted wisdom.

Shar thought as the fire started to catch. Nomgar would be dead by now, and he was yet one more whose blood was on her hands. It sickened her, but it could be no other way. To let enemies such as him live was to invite her own death, and worse, to strengthen the hands of the shamans in their tyranny over the people.

The fire roared to life, but within a little while the flames lowered and all the chiefs gathered round it in a circle. The two new chiefs that she had made took their place, as well as Asana, and Shar spoke to them.

"Make no mistake, the empire that was is being reborn. It's more than prophecy now. It's real, and it's happening, and when the tidings of this battle reach the shamans they will know fear. But it isn't enough."

The noise of the reveling army washed over the clearing, but no one seemed to hear it.

"What more can be done than we are already doing?" Sagadar asked.

"The shamans aren't just tyrants. They're sorcerers. Today, Kubodin and I managed to defeat them, but there were only two. In the future, more will come against us, and as we saw, they'll break all rules to defeat us, even using magic against men. We need magic of our own, with which we can defend or attack as necessary."

Nahring was going to answer, but she quietened him with a gesture.

"Let's state the problems first, and then we can tackle the solutions."

They agreed to this, and she went on. "Defending against attack by magic is a great concern, but we must also decide where to go next. That's not just a military decision. An army needs food and supplies, and going forward takes us a long way from the Wahlum Hills. We must also find ways to spread news of our victory as fast and as far as possible. That will sap the morale of any who would defy us, and at the same time encourage others to join us."

They nodded as she spoke. Most of them would already be thinking the same things.

"Think on those problems for a little while, and then we'll discuss your plans. While you're doing that, I shall write a letter."

"Who to?" Kubodin asked.

She smiled sweetly. "Why, to the shamans. I have a few things to say to them."

Kubodin's answering grin was wide. He, perhaps more than anyone, appreciated what she was going to do and the tone of the letter. In fact, she would draft it using the kind of impudence he was famous for.

She summoned a scribe and began to dictate the letter. None of the chiefs could hear what she said, but Kubodin kept glancing at her and grinning. And the scribe's hand began to shake.

All around them the noises of celebration grew louder. Shar could barely hear it though. Her mind was intent on what she was saying, and a few times even she thought she was going too far. Even so, she did not change the wording. Her purpose was to shock them, to unsettle them, to make them feel rage. In doing that, she might provoke them to act with haste and make poor decisions.

Battle was not won with swords alone, and the mind was a stronger, if more subtle, weapon than a steel blade.

26. The Seeds of Revenge

He stood on the top of the tower, and gazed upward. The sky was clear, and the stars looked down upon him. There was no beauty there, not for him. He may as well have stared into the cold and black heart of the void. It was all the same to his eyes.

It was said that celestial bodies foretold the future. He did not think so. Nevertheless, there was wisdom in the near-dark heavens for those who could discern it.

Change was coming. It was there in the pattern of the stars, and their movements. They did not say which clans would live nor die. Nor those that would prosper or decline. Nor even less if Shar Fei would triumph in battle, or if the shamans would vanquish her. But the pale glitter of their slow arc across the night gave warning. *The tide of destiny is rising high. Change ascends with it. The weak will fall, and the strong endure.*

He knew a time of change when he saw it. He was old enough. Old enough to have seen it before. Old enough to count centuries as the crumbs of time, and to take the measure of a millennia and say that he knew its beginning and would shape its end.

And he *would* shape its end. He cast his mind back to the beginning, and he saw Chen Fei. He loved him, and he despised him. The years had swept on since then, and the emperor was dust. For all his troubles, he had found the peace of death.

He himself was not so lucky. That peace eluded him, and he had to go on, whether he wished it or not. Yet still, a final release from his curse was within his grasp. He would reach for it, and if it bit him like a venomed snake he would still not let go. This time of change was *his*. He would make it so, and no power on earth could stop him.

He had waited a long time, but the swell of fate was now in his favor. He sat, and sipped of the wine in the golden goblet before him. The metal was cold to the touch. It gleamed and spoke of wealth, yet the wine was as ashes in his mouth. He ate cheese, sliced and perfectly placed on an engraved and shallow silver dish. It was dry as sand, and if it tasted of anything it was of the dust of tombs.

A long time he had lived. A long time the curse had deprived him of the simple pleasures of life. He had endured much to come to this point, and once death would have been a boon to him. Yet now he yearned for more. Revenge.

He neatly removed the cheese to the table, and emptied the wine into the silver platter. Magic was not his to command, not any significant kind anyway, yet he did have great skill with a scree dish. He was better at its uses than the shamans, and over the years he had found it often imperfect, but sometimes useful.

The wine stopped moving in the dish, and he drew his palm over it slowly uttering words of power. The engravings on its side began to move. The etchings were of serpents, and they slithered around the bowl, their little bodies growing darker than the silver of the dish as though it were blacked by fire in only the places they glided, and the red tongues in their mouths darted forward.

When his hand had passed over the liquid, there too something began to move. These were images, and he bent forward and looked intently.

He saw Shulu Gan, and the breath hissed from his mouth. How he hated her! Yet she looked old. Old, decrepit and near death. A fever was upon her, and her eyes darted anxiously. Almost it seemed that she looked straight up out of the bowl into his own eyes, but that could not be.

The vision of his enemy faded swiftly. Another replaced it. He saw Shar, the swords of legend in her hand and a battle raging all around her. He heard no sound, but faintly the wine rippled with the din of battle.

Perhaps she would die here, and his chances of victory with it. He wished her to live, for only thus could he prevail himself. Yet when she turned her head and he saw those violet eyes, the same that her forefather had, and even the cast of her face and the way she stood was like him, a low moan escaped his lips. He remembered what it was like to look into eyes like that. Eyes that bored into his soul.

No matter that she had his eyes, she was not the emperor. There was no reason to fear her. She turned away, her dark hair spraying out behind her, and she lifted her swords higher, and then the vision faded and she was soon gone.

He could not know if she lived or died, but she looked sure of herself. Whatever the outcome, he must wait patiently. A thousand years of whetting his revenge had taught him to do that though. He sat back and sighed.

All things would come to pass as they must. She would live, for a while at least. The shamans would scuttle about in fear, and he did not blame them. They thought this day would never come to pass, and unlike him they had not planned well for it. But that was good for him, and likewise that Shar was strong. While each of them was busy fighting the other, they would not pay attention to him, and that was the way he liked it. It was best to work from the shadows, and from the dark he would claim his victory. The enemy that was not seen was the one who prevailed.

The shamans had their weaknesses, and he had exploited them without the shamans even being aware. They did not know who he was. The girl was the same. She knew nothing of him, but he knew of her. And he knew she was prideful. That would be the trap to snare her.

He understood better than anyone the lure of power. It was subtle at first, but once it got a grip it never let go. It grew and grew, and each fulfillment only served to deepen the desire for more. Pride fueled it, and pride waxed with it. And Shar was a prideful girl already. It would trip her in the end, and he would be there to take advantage. It would drive her to make harsh decisions. At first they would be necessary, but soon she would forget herself and make decisions not for the benefit of the people but to increase her own supremacy.

She would be his to control when that happened, for he could offer her more. Shulu must die first though, else a warning could be given. Shulu once had the greatest power of all, but she had selflessly devoted herself to the emperor. She thought he was a good man, better than her, and worthy of it. She had been right.

That was nothing but the ghost of a memory though, forgotten even to most legends now. All that counted was the here and present, and *he* pulled the strings at the center of the web of the Cheng nation. The here and present was *his* to influence. And soon, through Shar, he would not just influence but command. His would be the voice that spoke through her lips. The shadow of his mind would rest over hers and shape her thoughts. Her lust for power would lead her to that, and the poisons and herbs that he knew, for it had been his task for hundreds of years to know such, would make her slow witted and malleable to his promptings.

He would control her, and through her the empire. He would teach her the greatness of her forefather who had sired her line, for he had known that man like no other, and she would thirst for that knowledge. No one had known him better, for had he not served him? Had he not once gone by the name of Olekhai, and been his prime minister?

Those had been days of glory. And days of dread. Never had he known a better time, or a worse. The shamans had offered him gold and power and influence, and foolishly he had accepted it and undertaken to do their bidding.

Poisoning the emperor had seemed so simple. He had not thought to feel such guilt though. But overlayed on everything now, seared into his soul, was the curse of Shulu after she had discovered his deed, and the flush of her magic as it entered into him. *I shall not kill you. Rather shall I give you life everlasting. Yet no man in the land will succor you. No man will be able to kill you. Nor will you be able to take your own life, though you will weary of it as a burden that cannot be borne. That which you eat will taste of ashes, and that which you drink will be as dust. Yet treachery will eat your heart, and neither peace nor comfort will you ever know.*

The memory of it was like fire in his blood, and every word of the curse had come true. Life everlasting, but without joy. Yet the endless days and sleepless nights had given him time to find a weakness in the curse and break it. *Regret for your wickedness will rend your soul until an emperor once more sits upon the throne.* That had also been part of the curse, and with Shar as emperor he would be free. And his vengeance would fall upon all his enemies, and when he had tasted of that sweetness and wrung all that he could out of life, he would lay himself down to die and at last know peace.

He sat back, for the door to the open-aired room moved and a servant entered. She was one of the new ones, and she came into the room meekly and said nothing. She was only a girl, younger even than Shar, and she came and silently removed the goblet and dish. As she moved the sleeve of her robe lifted and revealed the head of her snake tattoo. She hesitated a moment, for part of her training at this stage was to learn how to always hide it, but there was no need with him. She was an Ahat, and he was the Great Master of the Ahat Clan.

She left, moving silently and with grace. Young she might be, barely more than a child, but already she was deadly despite her size.

Olekhai smiled. The Ahat were a useful tool, and he was glad he had founded the clan. The wider world knew nothing of that though, or how the Ahat worked, or where their home was. Or who *he* was and what he wanted. Which was good. Because the knife in the dark from an unseen assailant always went home. And so would his schemes against Shar.

Thus ends *Swords of Defiance*. The Shaman's Sword series continues in book four, *Swords of Shadow*, where the challenges Shar faces mount, and the threat to the lands of the Cheng multiply…

SWORDS OF SHADOW

BOOK FOUR OF THE SHAMAN'S SWORD SERIES

COMING SOON!

Amazon lists millions of titles, and I'm glad you discovered this one. But if you'd like to know when I release a new book, instead of leaving it to chance, sign up for my new release list. I'll send you an email on publication.

Yes please! – Go to www.homeofhighfantasy.com and sign up.

No thanks – I'll take my chances.

Dedication

There's a growing movement in fantasy literature. Its name is noblebright, and it's the opposite of grimdark.

Noblebright celebrates the virtues of heroism. It's an old-fashioned thing, as old as the first story ever told around a smoky campfire beneath ancient stars. It's storytelling that highlights courage and loyalty and hope for the spirit of humanity. It recognizes the dark, the dark in us all, and the dark in the villains of its stories. It recognizes death, and treachery and betrayal. But it dwells on none of these things.

I dedicate this book, such as it is, to that which is noblebright. And I thank the authors before me who held the torch high so that I could see the path: J.R.R. Tolkien, C.S. Lewis, Terry Brooks, Susan Cooper, Roger Taylor and many others. I salute you.

And, for a time, I too shall hold the torch high.

Appendix: Encyclopedic Glossary

Note: The history of the Cheng Empire is obscure, for the shamans hid much of it. Yet the truth was recorded in many places and passed down in family histories, in secret societies and especially among warrior culture. This glossary draws on much of that 'secret' history, and each book in this series is individualized to reflect the personal accounts that have come down through the dark tracts of time to the main actors within each book's pages. Additionally, there is often historical material provided in its entries for people, artifacts and events that are not included in the main text.

Many races dwell in Alithoras. All have their own language, and though sometimes related to one another the changes sparked by migration, isolation and various influences often render these tongues unintelligible to each other.

The ascendancy of Halathrin culture across the land, who are sometimes called elves, combined with their widespread efforts to secure and maintain allies against various evil incursions, has made their language the primary means of communication between diverse peoples. This was especially so during the Shadowed Wars, but has persisted through the centuries afterward.

This glossary contains a range of names and terms. Some are of Halathrin origin, and their meaning is provided.

The Cheng culture is also revered by its people, and many names are given in their tongue. It is important to remember that the empire was vast though, and there is no one Cheng language but rather a multitude of dialects. Perfect consistency of spelling and meaning is therefore not to be looked for.

List of abbreviations:

Cam. Camar

Chg. Cheng

Comb. Combined

Cor. Corrupted form

Hal. Halathrin

Prn. Pronounced

Ahat: *Chg.* "Hawk in the night." A special kind of assassin. Used by the shamans in particular, but open for hire to anybody who can afford their fee. It is said that the shamans subverted an entire tribe in the distant past, and that every member of the community, from the children to the elderly, train to hone their craft at killing and nothing else. They grow no crops, raise no livestock nor pursue any trade save the bringing of death. The fees of their assignments pay for all their needs. This is legend only, for no such community has ever been found. But the lands of the Cheng are wide and such a community, if it exists, would be hidden and guarded.

Argash: *Chg.* "The clamor of war." A warrior of the Fen Wolf Tribe, and leader of one band of the leng-fah. His great-grandfather was once chief of the clan.

Asana: *Chg.* "Gift of light." Rumored to be the greatest swordmaster in the history of the Cheng people. His father was a Duthenor tribesman from outside the bounds of the old Cheng Empire.

Chen Fei: *Chg.* "Graceful swan." Swans are considered birds of wisdom and elegance in Cheng culture. It is said that one flew overhead at the time of Chen's birth, and his mother named him for it. He rose from poverty to become emperor of his people, and he was loved by many but despised by some. He was warrior, general, husband, father, poet, philosopher, painter, but most of all he was enemy to the machinations of the shamans who tried to secretly govern all aspects of the people.

Cheng: *Chg.* "Warrior." The overall name of the various related tribes united by Chen Fei. It was a word for warrior in his dialect, later adopted for his growing army and last of all for the people of his nation. His empire disintegrated after his assassination, but much of the culture he fostered endured.

Cheng Empire: A vast array of realms formerly governed by kings and united, briefly, under Chen Fei. One of the largest empires ever to rise in Alithoras.

Dakashul: *Chg.* "Stallion of two colors – a piebald." Chief of the Iron Dog Clan.

Drasta: *Chg.* "Ice." Shaman of the Two Ravens Clan.

Drubadar: *Chg.* "Ox in the fields." A warrior of the Wahlum Hills.

Eagle Claw Mountains: A mountain range toward the south of the Cheng Empire. It is said the people who later became the Cheng lived here first and over centuries moved out to populate the surrounding lands. Others believe that these people were blue-eyed, and intermixed with various other races as they came down off the mountains to trade and make war.

Elù-haraken: *Hal.* "The shadowed wars." Long ago battles in a time that is become myth to the Cheng tribes.

Fen Wolf Tribe: A tribe that live in Tsarin Fen. Once, they and the neighboring Soaring Eagle Tribe were one people and part of a kingdom. It is also told that Chen Fei was born in that realm.

Fields of Rah: Rah signifies "ocean of the sky" in many Cheng dialects. It is a country of vast grasslands but at its center is Nagrak City, which of old was the capital of the empire. It was in this city that the emperor was assassinated.

Forest of Dreams: A forest in the northwest of the Cheng lands. Sometimes said to be haunted, but certainly known to be the dwelling place of many creatures of magic driven out of more populated lands. A place of danger that even shamans avoid.

Gan: *Chg.* "They who have attained." It is an honorary title added to a person's name after they have acquired great skill. It can be applied to warriors, shamans, sculptors, weavers or any particular expertise. It is reserved for the greatest of the best.

Ghirlock: *Chg.* "The goat that flies." A bird of the snipe species. Associated with the supernatural and the elemental gods of the Cheng. Its sound in flight is like the bleat of a goat.

Green Hornet Clan: A grassland clan immediately to the west of the Wahlum Hills. Their numbers are relatively small, but they are famous for their use of venomed arrows and especially darts.

Great Master: Title for the chief of the Ahat Clan. His real name is known to few, and used by none.

Halathrin: *Hal.* "People of Halath." A race of elves named after an honored lord who led an exodus of his people to the land of Alithoras in pursuit of justice, having sworn to defeat a great evil. They are human, though of fairer form, greater skill and higher culture. They possess a unity of body, mind and spirit that enables insight and endurance beyond the native races of Alithoras. Said to be immortal, but killed in great numbers during their conflicts in ancient times with the evil they sought to destroy. Those conflicts are collectively known as the Shadowed Wars.

Heart of the Hurricane: The shamans' term for the state of mind warriors call Stillness in the Storm. See that term for further information.

Huigar: *Chg.* "Mist on the mountain peak." A bodyguard to Shar. Daughter of the chief of the Smoking Eyes Clan, and a swordsperson of rare skill.

Iron Dog Clan: A tribe of the Wahlum Hills. So named for their legendary endurance and determination.

Kubodin: *Chg.* Etymology unknown. A wild warrior from the Wahlum Hills, and chief of the Two Ravens Clan. Simple appearing, but far more than he seems. Asana's manservant and friend.

Kuthondrin: *Chg.* Etymology unknown. Brother to Kubodin.

Lasalath: *Chg.* "Lone cloud." Chief of the Soaring Eagle Clan. Once a nazram before unexpectedly inheriting the chieftainship after his father and older brother were assassinated. The tribe's shaman was suspected of arranging it, but Lasalath could prove nothing.

Leng-fah: *Chg.* "Wolf skills." An organization of warrior scouts who patrol the borders of Tsarin Fen to protect its people from hostile incursions by other tribes. They take their name from the swamp wolf, a creature of great stealth and cunning. This is the totem animal of the Fen Wolf Tribe.

Lòhren: *Hal. Prn.* Ler-ren. "Knowledge giver – a counselor." Other terms used by various nations include sage, wizard, and druid.

Magic: Mystic power.

Nahaz: *Chg.* "White fire." A spirit fermented from mare's milk. Originated in the Nagrak Tribe, but traded throughout the tribes. Said to possess recuperative powers, and used in many rituals.

Nahring: *Chg.* "White on the lake – mist." Chief of the Smoking Eyes Clan, and father of Huigar. Rumor persists that his family possesses some kind of magic, but if so it has never been publicly revealed.

Nagrak: *Chg.* "Those who follow the herds." A Cheng tribe that dwell on the Fields of Rah. Traditionally they lived a nomadic lifestyle, traveling in the wake of herds of wild cattle that provided all their needs. But an element of their tribe, and some contend this was another tribe in origin that they conquered, are great builders and live in a city.

Nagrak City: A city at the heart of the Fields of Rah. Once the capital of the Cheng Empire.

Nakatath: *Chg.* "Emperor-to-be." A term coined by Chen Fei and used by him during the period where he sought to bring the Cheng tribes together into one nation. It is said that it deliberately mocked the shamans, for they used the term *Nakolbrin* to signify an apprentice shaman ready to ascend to full authority.

Namrodin: *Chg.* Etymology unknown. A warrior of the Two Ravens Tribe.

Nassring: *Chg.* "Ice on the lake." Chief of the Green Hornet Clan.

Nazram: *Chg.* "The wheat grains that are prized after the chaff is excluded." An elite warrior organization that is in service to the shamans. For the most part, they are selected from those who quest for the twin swords each triseptium, though there are exceptions to this.

Nerchak: *Chg.* "Hollow tooth." A young man who befriends Shar. His name is also a term for jewelry made from the teeth, horns or tusks of dangerous animals that are strung into a necklace or bracelet. In some dialects, the word is spelled "nerchek" and is a euphemism for venomous snakes.

Night Walker Clan: A tribe of the Wahlum Hills. The name derives from their totem animal, which is a nocturnal predator of thick forests. It's a type of cat, small but fierce and covered in black fur.

Nomgar: *Chg.* "Tree that pierces the forest canopy." Chief of the Fen Wolf Tribe.

Olekhai: *Chg.* "The falcon that plummets." A famous and often used name in the old world before, and during, the Cheng Empire. Never used since the assassination of the emperor, however. The most prominent bearer of the name during the days of the emperor was the chief of his council of wise men. He was, essentially, prime minister of the emperor's government. But he betrayed his lord and his people. Shulu Gan spared his life, but only so as to punish him with a terrible curse.

Quest of Swords: Occurs every triseptium to mark the three times seven years the shamans lived in exile during the emperor's life. The best warriors of each clan seek the twin swords of the emperor. Used by the shamans as a means of finding the most skilled warriors in the land and recruiting them to their service.

Rackgar: *Chg.* "Literally means spear tall – a tall pole carrying a banner." A warrior of the Wahlum Hills.

Radatan: *Chg.* "The ears that flick – a slang term for deer." A hunter of the Two Ravens Clan.

Running Bear Clan: A tribe of the Wahlum Hills. Their totem is a species of small bear that inhabits the hills.

Sagadar: *Chg.* "Willow tree." Chief of the Night Walker Clan.

Shadowed Wars: See Elù-haraken.

Shapechanger: Prominent figures in Cheng legend and history. They are beings able to take any form, and are renowned for being mischievous. Other stories, or histories, claim they are creatures of evil in servitude to the shamans.

Shaman: The religious leaders of the Cheng people. They are sorcerers, and though the empire is fragmented they work as one across the lands to serve their own united purpose. Their spiritual home is Three Moon Mountain, but few save shamans have ever been there.

Shar: *Chg.* "White stone – the peak of a mountain." A young woman of the Fen Wolf Tribe. Claimed by Shulu Gan to be the descendent of Chen Fei.

Shulu Gan: *Chg.* The first element signifies "magpie." A name given to the then leader of the shamans for her hair was black, save for a streak of white that ran through it.

Skaaghul: *Chg.* "Sun-bleached bones." Shaman to the Fen Wolf Clan.

Smoking Eyes Clan: A tribe of the Wahlum Hills. Named for a god, who they take as their totem.

Soaring Eagle Tribe: A tribe that borders the Fen Wolf clan. At one time, one with them, but now, as is the situation with most tribes, hostilities are common. The eagle is their totem, for the birds are plentiful in the mountain lands to the south and often soar far from their preferred habitat over the tribe's grasslands.

Stillness in the Storm: The state of mind a true warrior seeks in battle. Neither angry nor scared, neither hopeful nor worried. When emotion is banished from the mind, the body is free to express the skill acquired through long years of training. Sometimes also called Calmness in the Storm or the Heart of the Hurricane.

Swimming Osprey Clan: A tribe of the Wahlum Hills. Their totem is the osprey, often seen diving into the ocean to catch fish.

Taga Nashu: *Chg.* "The Grandmother who does not die." One of the many epithets of Shulu Gan, greatest of the shamans but cast from their order.

Tarok: *Chg.* "Head of a deer above tall grass." A warrior of the Soaring Eagle Tribe. Once a nazram, but he left that order of warriors.

Three Moon Mountain: A mountain in the Eagle Claw range. Famed as the home of the shamans. None know what the three moons reference relates to except, perhaps, the shamans.

Triseptium: A period of three times seven years. It signifies the exiles of the shamans during the life of the emperor. Declared by the shamans as a cultural treasure, and celebrated by them. Less so by the tribes, but the shamans encourage it. Much more popular now than in past ages.

Tsarin Fen: *Chg.* Tsarin, which signifies mountain cat, was a general under Chen Fei. It is said he retired to the swamp after the death of his leader. At one time, many regions and villages were named after generals, but the shamans changed the names and did all they could to make people forget the old ones. In their view, all who served the emperor were criminals and their achievements were not to be celebrated. Tsarin Fen is one of the few such names that still survive.

Two Ravens Clan: A tribe of the Wahlum Hills. Their totem is the raven.

Uhrum: *Chg.* "The voice that sings the dawn." Queen of the gods.

Wahlum Hills: *Chg. Comb. Hal.* "Mist-shrouded highlands." Hills to the north-west of the old Cheng empire, and home to Kubodin.

About the author

I'm a man born in the wrong era. My heart yearns for faraway places and even further afield times. Tolkien had me at the beginning of *The Hobbit* when he said, ". . . one morning long ago in the quiet of the world . . ."

Sometimes I imagine myself in a Viking mead-hall. The long winter night presses in, but the shimmering embers of a log in the hearth hold back both cold and dark. The chieftain calls for a story, and I take a sip from my drinking horn and stand up . . .

Or maybe the desert stars shine bright and clear, obscured occasionally by wisps of smoke from burning camel dung. A dry gust of wind marches sand grains across our lonely campsite, and the wayfarers about me stir restlessly. I sip cool water and begin to speak.

I'm a storyteller. A man to paint a picture by the slow music of words. I like to bring faraway places and times to life, to make hearts yearn for something they can never have, unless for a passing moment.